ATTACHMENT THEORY

ATTACHMENT THEORY

FLINDERS UNIVERSITY
CREATIVE WRITING ANTHOLOGY

Edited by:
Travis Abrook, Jesse Allan, Rachel Bauer, Penny
Foster, Ez Knill, Maddy Nyp, Hayden Thomas and
Gavin Vouriot
with
Lynette Washington

First published by Glimmer Press 2025
West Beach, South Australia
www.glimmerpress.com.au

 A catalogue record for this
book is available from the
National Library of Australia

ISBN: 978-0-646-71791-3

Cover images by Abby Guy
Cover design by Abby Guy
Internal images by Abby Guy
Internal design by Lynette Washington

Printed in Australia

To Amy, to Sean, and to each other.

We live and work on the traditional lands of the
Kaurna people of Kaurna Yerta. We pay our respect
to Elders past and present. This always was and will
be Aboriginal land.

Contents

Introduction

In our third year as BCA students at Flinders University, we were given the incredible opportunity to create and write our own anthology of short stories to be published. The opportunity to be published at the end of our undergrad years is a uniquely terrifying reward for our work in this degree. As writers we studied here to hone our skills and meet like-minded students, so to reach a point where our work will be published outside the boundaries of the university is an exciting prospect that we are extraordinarily grateful for, despite the intense workload such an undertaking encompasses.

We came together on our first day of class, standing with fear, but also with determination. With our different backgrounds, our different writing skills, and our different genre preferences, we all had to undertake a difficult task in coming together and deciding on an idea. The overwhelming and daunting journey ahead frightened us, and we cried and screamed into the sky. But then, we remembered how fortunate we were to have compassionate friends, who would stop at nothing to ensure we got through this journey together. Anthology students of the past visited us, and they gave us incredible advice.

Our first drafts filled us with excitement, inspiration, and a little anxiety. Okay, a *lot* of anxiety. We were feeling the pressure of this not only being our eventual major assignment, but also our first debuts as published authors. We all were feeling the stress of wanting to make these unformed stories into someone uniquely us, and something that would represent who we are as authors. The first round of workshopping was nerve wracking. Sure, most of us had done workshopping with each other before, but this felt different, more intense. This round felt like a perfect icebreaker for us to lay out everything and see what could and would work for us.

Our book began as a series of stories following the reincarnation of the same two souls, exploring the relationships they develop throughout their lifespans together. We were three hours into deliberating who, or what, would be reincarnating these two souls, when *The* Sean Williams joined our meeting. After listening in for a while, he suggested that the additional narrative of reincarnation was creating too much extra work, and our linking theme of 'love in all its forms' was strong enough on its own, backing up Jess' previous suggestion. After a short freak-out we all agreed to drop the reincarnation element, however all our stories still take place throughout human history—or in the future—and focus on the relationship between two people. (Or cats. Or wolves).

For most of us, the city campus was a mystical, unknown land, where you selected the floor outside the elevators, and they didn't go to the ground floor for some reason. It was there that we first met the wonderful Lynette in person. After awkward introductions were over, we acknowledged the existence of the style guide and promptly ignored it for our own sanity, and discussed our roles such as marketing, editing, design and the undersong correspondence. We summarised our stories, but still couldn't provide a title for the anthology; a problem which would haunt us 'til the very end. At least we had more of an idea for the book cover for the spectacularly talented Abby to consider. We concluded the meeting with a timeline of the next year or two, a long, intimidating and yet exciting road ahead, and recorded some marketing content for social media.

In the aftermath of the hell that was submitting our final assignments, the team began meeting bi-weekly to line edit our short stories in preparation for sending our manuscript to Glimmer Press. This fiddly process included booking out Flinders Uni's movie room and throwing our stories up on the big screen, then combing through word-by-word to find errors. Some meetings were filled with regrettable jokes (shoutout to Gavin's character Sir Paul, who derailed many the editing session), some were borderline wars (three years of university and we still do not understand the Oxford comma) but somehow, we persevered, tumbling out with a polished manuscript ready to be sent away.

Settling on the title was our greatest hurdle. Everything we came up with felt cliché or 'already done.' A temporary placeholder was found but the only issue was that it applied to our *previous* theme (reincarnation). So, our meetings continued — consisting of splattering words on a whiteboard, to then shuffle out with nothing agreed upon, except for the fact we didn't have a title. Our patience was growing thin. Eventually, Travis suggested 'attachment issues.' This was the strongest divider. Thankfully, we did all agree the word attachment had to be in the title, and from this a variation became: 'attachment theory.'

The acknowledgements were written in one sitting — that was the easy part. The hard part was working out the finer points of our introduction. As we all wanted to take part in the process of writing it, we had to come up with a way to collaborate and write a cohesive foreword to our anthology. We held many meetings, all of us spread out over a table with laptops and notebooks, trying to stay on task as we laughed over all of the inside jokes that we'd started over the course of our years working together. Eventually we landed on what you're reading now, an insight into our group and process that we're all pretty proud of.

Looking back on our journey, I can't help but picture our manuscript as a lotus flower. After countless long days and late nights where it felt like we were digging ourselves deeper into the mud, we finally reached a point where our stories felt whole. However, while you may think finalising the manuscript was the easy part, I think we underestimated just how much time would go into making sure every single story was formatted correctly. After many hours filled with blood, sweat, and tears, the manuscript finally bloomed into a completed anthology, and we sent it off to the publisher filled with nerves and excitement for our next chapter in this journey.

With our manuscript finished we couldn't be more excited to finally share our work with the world. In the end, it was a long and arduous journey, but we made it. So, from all of us, we hope you enjoy these ten stories of attachment.

Love is a Battlefield

Gavin Vouriot

The Kingdoms of Alberic and Fausten, England – 750 A.D.

In the darkest time of the Dark Ages, which ironically isn't midnight, England was split into the heptarchy, seven Anglo-Saxon kingdoms that would eventually unify. Countless history books can recount the goings on in Dark Ages England, but none speak of the minor war between the lost eighth and ninth kingdoms, Alberic and Fausten. The two kingdoms were constantly in conflict for petty reasons, but a temporary peace was formed when Queen Lorraine of Alberic and King Siegwulf of Fausten put their people first and abolished conflict between them. Any readers paying attention would have noticed the word *temporary* in the previous sentence. Peace and isolation were not words in the limited dictionary of two young lovers, split apart by the treaty signed by the kingdoms they were heirs to. Conflict is an unremarkable notion, but in the pantheon of wars, this one is notable in how it concluded, for it may be one of the only times in history where love truly conquered all.

Between usurping the throne of her kingdom from her mother, declaring war on Fausten, and turning twenty-one, Charlotte of Alberic was confident that this was going to be the happiest day of her life.

What swelled her heart most was her proposal to her husband-to-be, Prince Alexander of Fausten. On the list of her day's activities, it was at the very top, right above sending her mother to the dungeons and getting in a morning pamper before she rode off to war, both of which were crossed off.

Usurping the throne shattered the peace treaty between Alberic and Fausten, which was good riddance in Charlotte's eyes. Any treaty that forbade her from seeing her true love was a bad treaty indeed. Their parents never approved of their relationship, something about their families being sworn enemies. If that meant a bit of war had to be waged, at least Charlotte had plans for the rest of the day. Living peacefully had been so dull for her.

Charlotte stood on the crest of a muddy hill, overlooking Castle Fausten below, dressed in a suit of magnificent armour. Her army was behind her: a good two-hundred men waiting for the signal to charge. Fausten was doing the same in front of their castle, rallying their ranks and arming catapults, though their ruler was nowhere to be seen (at first sign of the coming battle, King Siegwulf busied himself with locking his son Alexander away in the castle's tallest tower, forcing the lad to watch the battle from afar, which would have been awful if not for the platter of bread and cheeses he was given).

Both armies waited nervously for the other to act first. Given the long peace between kingdoms, many of the soldiers were new to battle, and quite shy about the idea of clashing swords. War is a social activity, after all.

Fausten started first, screaming out an unsure battle cry before advancing towards Charlotte's army. As the Fausten legion approached, Charlotte held her sword steady, ready for the howl of war from her kingdom's oldest and most decorated knight, Sir Paul, who was stationed alongside her at the front of the army.

The legendary knight commander sat upon his brilliant white steed, Sir Paul III, his sword unsheathed and pointed towards the heavens, as if pricking the rosy butt-cheeks of God. He was buck naked apart from his gauntlets.

Sir Paul was a master of the battlefield, though that was before the relentless conflict drove him insane. Nowadays, he was a liability, as cannibals usually are, but being new to war herself, Charlotte decided to let Sir Paul lead the Alberic soldiers at the front of the army (good military strategy notes that the element of surprise is always a worthwhile tactic, and there is no better surprise than a naked madman with a taste for human flesh).

'—with glory, might, and daffodils, we march towards victory under the Alberic banner!' Sir Paul yelled. 'Now is the deciding time, for today is when we crush the Fausten name and feast upon their throats and livers...'

Charlotte impatiently twisted her sword. The old man was taking too long to rally the troops. As important as the battle to unify the kingdoms was,

Charlotte only cared about being with Alexander. Unity was just a convenient bonus.

'—so let us march towards uneaten flesh, my brave daffodils!' Sir Paul screamed. 'Advance and—'

An arrow struck the knight's head before he could finish. He fell off his horse and into a pool of thick mud.

'Bollocks,' Charlotte said. The knights around Charlotte seemed unsure of what to do in response. She looked expectantly to the man next to her, Sir Bentley, her personal knight and royal guard. 'Why aren't our soldiers advancing?' she asked.

'Because they're stupid,' Bentley said. 'They respond well to grand speeches, but if one is left unfinished, their bloodlust conveniently vanishes.'

She sighed. 'Time for another plan.'

To Bentley's shock, Charlotte abandoned his side and rushed towards Sir Paul's white steed, taking the reins. Forgoing a rousing speech, she kicked the horse's sides and rode towards the Fausten soldiers. She tore the helmet off her head, letting her long locks fly free against the battering wind, flustering the hearts of every man on the battlefield.

'Defend the Queen!' a voice called from her army which stirred her soldiers into action. If they wouldn't fight with their hearts, Charlotte thought it prudent to use their dicks instead.

After shaking away their own blushes, the Fausten soldiers began their attack. Archers fired volleys of arrows towards the Alberic Queen as she and Sir Paul III barrelled through their ranks.

A boulder fired from the nearest Fausten catapult. It sailed over Charlotte, landing in the centre of her army's ranks. She hoped Bentley managed to escape before he was crushed. Her guilt for leaving him behind quickly faded when the sight of a few Fausten soldiers rolling two shapely boulders together to arm the catapult reminded her of Alexander and his glorious loins.

With the Fausten castle gates closed, she needed another way inside. The catapult looked promising. She rode towards the pesky weapon, a dangerous plan forming.

Her assault was complicated when a stray Fausten arrow struck Sir Paul III right in its arse. The white stallion reared on its hind legs and threw her off, flinging her onto another conveniently placed pile of mud (the main reason this era is referred to as the Dark Ages is precisely because *everything* was covered in mud).

A group of Fausten soldiers surrounded the injured horse.

'No!' Charlotte screamed. 'Get away from him!'

To the Fausten soldiers, what seemed like a hysteric girl crying out for the safety of her horse was in fact a warning intended for their ears. They learned their lesson the hard way as Sir Paul III chomped a soldier's head off and then proceeded to bite into the others as they ran away (in his madness, Sir Paul had a bad habit of feeding his steed the corpses of his enemies). The stallion dashed off to the heart of the battlefield, pursuing its next meal, leaving Charlotte alone to assault the catapult.

Soldiers advanced towards her as she rushed to the weapon. Charlotte cut each down into gruesome chunks. She gleefully sliced every enemy apart, making sure to change her techniques as to not get bored, switching between beheading, disembowelling, and a technique so shocking even the most brutal of bastards would get in a hissy about if it was performed in front of them.

While Charlotte was a one-woman-army, Fausten's vast numbers meant reinforcements were always on the horizon. The castle seemed to house an infinite number of Siegwulf's soldiers, and while Charlotte could confidently kill hundreds of men, everyone had a limit of how many trained killers they could take on at once.

'Blimey, that's a lot,' she muttered as a few dozen large knights sauntered towards her.

Backup came in the nick of time, in the form of Sir Bentley and his team of knights that Charlotte hadn't bothered to learn the names of. They tore through the Fausten reinforcements, Bentley positioning himself to fight at his Queen's side.

'This is insanity, Your Majesty!' Bentley yelled, parrying a blow. 'I didn't ask questions when you usurped your mother, nor when you charged into the fray by yourself, but I certainly need an explanation to why you are out front of the Fausten castle, eyeing the catapult like it's a prospective bedfellow!'

'The truth,' Charlotte said proudly, 'is that I intend to ask Prince Alexander for his hand in marriage.'

'But he's the enemy!'

'I love him, Bentley.' She shook her head wistfully. 'You wouldn't understand.'

'I perfectly understand stupidity when I see it. We need to get you back to the castle. There are plenty of good Alberic suitors waiting for your hand in marriage. Much better choices than the prince of our *enemy.*'

'You're sounding like my mother now. Always trying to meddle in my love life. "Oh, look here, Charlotte. Here's a nice, strapping man for you to marry, Charlotte. He's very handsome and comes from a family known for having many kids, Charlotte." Yes, perhaps he is a good match, if you enjoy imbecile peasants with missing teeth and pink eye!'

Bentley nodded nervously, knowing full well that Charlotte had a few things to work through.

Amid their discussion, one of Bentley's soldiers was cut down by a Fausten knight. Bentley ordered his troops into a circular formation around Charlotte, who nudged her way through to stand alongside them, a little too eager to fight (Bentley wasn't fond of the excited gleam in her eyes).

'Majesty, you are not safe out here!' Bentley yelled, bashing someone away with a shield.

'Is that concern, or your own cowardice I hear?' Charlotte huffed, disembowelling someone.

'Please, Your Majesty, I am thinking only of your safety,' Bentley said, deflecting an attack.

'If you really want me safe, quit complaining and follow my lead,' Charlotte said, pulling a Fausten soldier's still-beating heart out from his punctured chest. 'I have a plan.'

'That's never a good sign,' Bentley grunted, blocking an attack. He found it best not to argue with her when she got in one of these moods. 'I will follow you wherever, my Queen, even if I don't condone your choice of husband.'

Charlotte smiled at Bentley as blood from an enemy soldier's slit neck sprayed onto her face. 'Glad that's settled.'

'But if the castle gate is down, how do you propose to get inside?'

After heaving her blade from a kebab of corpses, Charlotte pointed to the catapult a few yards away.

'I fear you may be insane, Majesty,' Bentley muttered.

Charlotte shrugged and took off, Bentley and his men joining her. They sliced through the soldiers in their way, desperately racing to the weapon before it could fire another boulder. Charlotte leaped onto the wooden frame, fuelled by adrenaline and a vague plan that seemed more ridiculous every step she took along the catapult's beam.

Bentley was too horrified to look, cleaving his way through the operators before they could fire. But he wasn't fast enough. The payload was ready to be released.

Charlotte increased her speed. She stepped onto the boulder as it fired, and when the bucket's angle aligned with the height of the Fausten ramparts, she leaped into the air, narrowly avoiding taking off with the boulder. To those below, Charlotte looked like an angel, soaring through the air against the light of the sun breaking through the dreary, ash-coloured sky. In mid-air, Charlotte swung her blade, ready to cut down the soldiers in awe of her on the ramparts below. She landed in a mess of blood and metal, screaming a battle cry that did little to hide the elation she felt slicing into flesh.

She ran along the ramparts towards the gatehouse, dodging Fausten blades as they arced towards her. One soldier blocked the way inside, so she threw herself into him and crashed the door down. The soldiers guarding the winch were shocked to find a woman invading their gatehouse, but they were even more surprised to discover their intestines on the floor a second later.

With newfound strength born from her killing spree, Charlotte operated the winch and raised the front gate, allowing Bentley and his men entry into the heart of the enemy kingdom. With their backup, she could storm the castle proper and hopefully make it to wherever Alexander was being held.

She wondered how he was doing, and if he was fighting as hard as she to claim the life they both yearned so heavily for.

At this point in the story there would normally be an exciting interlude detailing Alexander's perspective, namely what he was doing during all this stuff about catapults, man-eating horses, and Charlotte being an unstoppable force of nature. While the author would like to elaborate on his story, he felt it would be unfair on Alexander to detail his escapades on the royal toilet.

It is quite disgusting, and honestly, not a laughing matter (the author recommends looking elsewhere for detailed accounts of bowel movements).

Yes, Alexander was stuck on the toilet during most of the battle (likely the work of one of those dastardly cheeses). Fortunately, when he does make his formal appearance in this story, he has cleaned himself up and doesn't smell too bad. For now, Charlotte's thrilling battle for love continues.

When Sir Bentley found Charlotte in the Fausten castle courtyard, she was in the middle of washing the blood out of her hair using water she found in a pail formally held by a servant boy she had accidently killed. He wasn't using the water anymore.

'What in God's name are you doing?' Bentley yelled.

'I have to look nice for Alexander,' Charlotte said, wondering why Bentley had asked such a stupid question. 'Do you have a hairbrush on you?'

'Of course not!'

One of Bentley's knights stepped forward and handed her his. 'I thank thee,' Charlotte said and immediately started brushing the knots out.

As she groomed herself, Charlotte lingered on thoughts of her and Alexander. The love they shared was deep and passionate. Since they met during peace talks between their kingdoms, several quiet nights had been stolen in favour of some fabulous lovemaking away from prying eyes. They shared their dreams and doubts with one another, regularly talking until their throats were dry.

Charlotte loved Alexander like no other man in her life. It was a love so strong it gave her the power to fight like a beast against anyone that opposed it.

If only their parents felt the same.

Queen Lorraine of Alberic and King Siegwulf of Fausten ruined their chances at a life together by putting the needs of their kingdoms above their own. In their youth, they were much like Charlotte and Alexander, forgoing arrangements and tradition to sate their lust for each other. But the potential unification of their kingdoms meant they would be a greater enemy to their budding invaders: Essex, Wessex, and Kent, who had otherwise left the two kingdoms alone to squabble amongst themselves for land that held no tactical advantage to anyone. Neither monarch could risk the danger that would befall their kingdoms in exchange for true love and unity (or hot, sweaty nights entangled with each other under a curtain of bedsheets, performing acts of passion so extreme even the most devilish of deviants would squirm in discomfort). For long-lasting peace, they believed their children should make a similar sacrifice.

Charlotte thought that sounded like a boring way to live her life.

After fighting their way through the castle, Charlotte and her small band reached the castle's reception hall. The door to the throne room was blocked by a group of soldiers in black armour led by King Siegwulf himself, brandishing two short swords in his hands (though he insisted they were average sized).

'Queen Charlotte!' he yelled. 'I know why you've come here. You insist on shattering the peace your mother and I worked so hard to create. Your crusade ends here, my dear, for I shall cut you down with the silver of my blades!'

'How dare you raise your sword against a Queen!' Charlotte yelled. 'Have you no shame?'

'You are no Queen,' Siegwulf asserted. 'Your mother, Lorraine, is the true ruler of Alberic, a harbinger of peace worth fighting for. I have great respect for her. You, a demon in human flesh, have earned none of it.'

'Hmm? What was that?' Charlotte found her thoughts drifting elsewhere while Siegwulf was talking, mainly going through ideas for her and Alexander's wedding.

King Siegwulf's face went red. 'I was saying, your mother is—'

'You dare try and insult my mother?'

'No! You arrogant woman, I was saying—'

'I put her in the dungeons, by the by. Seizing the throne was purely a professional disagreement, so I didn't see the need to kill her. I can offer you the same fate, King Something-Or-Other Wolf.

The King's face contorted in a fit of red rage. 'Screw formalities! I won't rest until you're dead in the ground!'

The King threw himself at Charlotte, the rest of his elite guard following suit. Both sides clashed in a fury of clanging metal and spattering crimson. The King's guards outclassed Bentley's soldiers, who each fell to Fausten steel in the most dramatic ways possible. Bentley managed to cut one of Siegwulf's knights down, while Charlotte severed another man's head from his neck, resulting in a glorious fountain of red.

Charlotte went for the Fausten king, who lunged at her with his two lowly blades. He nicked her several times when she tried to dodge, but she parried most of his attacks. She lured a desperate swing from Siegwulf, making him accidently stab one of his own soldiers when she dodged. With his blade stuck in his own man's back, Charlotte unleashed her wrath upon Siegwulf, cleaving both of his arms away with two brutal slashes before kicking him down into a puddle of his own blood.

The king's defeat was a short-lived victory as the rest of the Fausten army seemed to realise Charlotte was in their castle, for they were charging through the halls towards her. Bentley stood his ground as the army approached.

'Go to him, Your Majesty!' he yelled. 'Find Alexander! You mean the world to me, Queen Charlotte, and while I can't condone or stomach your methods sometimes, I respect you a great deal. You're my friend, and I want the very best for you, so make damn well sure you unite the land and marry your true love. Don't let my sacrifice be in vain!'

But Charlotte was already halfway through the door before he finished.

Inside, the throne room was pure chaos. Soldiers hacked away at each other, all wearing Fausten colours (in a bid to keep his son imprisoned, King Siegwulf had set his men upon those loyal to Alexander, resulting in further conflict within).

Amid the anarchy, Charlotte found Alexander standing around without an opponent to fight. He had his (*exceptionally*) long sword drawn, but seemed to shy away from conflict, like one would do when presented with a plate of nasty cheese. For some reason his trousers were also partly undone, but Charlotte decided to ignore that for now. They met each other's eyes, both lighting up at the sight. In unison, the lovers sprinted towards each other, becoming twin sparks of bliss within a mess of bloody chaos.

Siegwulf's soldiers tried to intervene. They came at Charlotte, but she furiously cut down any that approached, dodging the peskier ones that didn't die immediately. She slid underneath the legs of a tall knight and rolled to her feet, while Alexander clumsily tripped his way out from the direction of a lethal strike.

'Not on my watch!' a muffled voice screamed. King Siegwulf, ghostly pale, with arms reduced to dripping stumps, ran up behind Charlotte with a puny dagger held in his teeth.

She looked to Alexander, who was still running. Two soldiers blocked her way, and Siegwulf was getting closer. She ran towards the men, who were both readying their blades to strike. They swung, and she jumped. With the lightest step, her foot bounced off one of the swords, which led into a powerful kick, knocking one of the soldiers away. She rolled towards Alexander, landing perfectly on one knee and took his hand.

'Prince Alexander of Fausten, will you marry me?'

He gave her a large smile. 'It would be my highest honour, Queen Charlotte of Alberic.'

Suddenly, the fighting ceased.

'A union!' someone yelled from afar.

Cheering erupted inside the throne room. Two knights, who were in the middle of stabbing each other, turned and wished the couple congratulations, blood spilling from both their mouths.

With the proposal final, there was no more need for conflict. The two kingdoms would become one.

Royal messengers that were previously hiding from the bloodshed dashed out of the throne room and relayed the news to the rest of the battlefield (though the saner ones ran all the way out the kingdom and never looked back).

Charlotte and Alexander took each other's hands and led a parade of cheering knights out of the castle to announce their marriage to the greater battlefield. King Siegwulf was left behind, ignored by everyone and bewildered by the events that just occurred, eventually bleeding out and dying alone inside the empty throne room.

As the couple continued their march, Charlotte halted momentarily when they walked into the reception hall. A mess of corpses was around them, among the pile Sir Bentley. She froze, unable to tear herself away from the gruesome sight.

'What is wrong, my sweet?' Alexander asked. 'The battle is over, my dreadful father is dead, and we are to be married. Why is your face painted with such gloom?'

She stared deeply into the eyes of Bentley's decapitated head before turning and flashing one of her perfect smiles at her husband-to-be. 'Oh, it's just these corpses. Can we get them cleared out before we continue walking? I'd hate to further stain my boots.'

Later that evening, once the battlefield was empty of all fury, Charlotte and Alexander walked along the ramparts of Castle Fausten, holding each other tightly. They gazed into the rising moonlight that illuminated the blood-soaked hill their kingdoms had fought upon. The land was beautiful at this hour. The atmosphere of the night was palpable, from the moonlight glistening off the armour of hundreds of corpses, the sweet stench of blood on the air, and the distant screams of stragglers on the battlefield being chased by Sir Paul III, his bloodthirsty neigh chilling the already cool air.

'We may have united our kingdoms,' Alexander said, 'but it is not an end to war. Our unity means the other seven kingdoms will see us as a viable threat now. There will be more fighting, more bloodshed.'

'I don't care,' Charlotte said, leaning her head against his shoulder. 'I'm with you, and that's all that matters.'

Alexander pressed a kiss against his betrothed's forehead. 'Then all is well.'

Under the Wolf's Gaze

Travis Abrook

Northumbria – 956

My dearest son, sit around our blazing fire and lean against Rory. Search deep and focus on my voice. Listen closely to my tale.

In a world new to us in Northumbria, the Danes had just formed the city of York, and we held a farmstead not too far away. I was a young boy with straw hair that laid around my shoulder like my mother's did. I hardly remember the face of my father, who died through the conquering of the realm of Northumbria. So, I formed a strong bond with my mother, who also fought in those battles, but she had at least returned to me.

Unfortunately, this tale begins on the day when a blade leaked my mother's blood, burning the snow below me; it was pointed sharp, only a few inches from slicing my neck.

I felt the dread eat away at my body, accepting my return to my mother's clutches, not in this life but in the next. But I wouldn't be telling you this story if that blade had sliced me.

Thus, when a beast of white cloud descended like a Valkyrie from Valhalla, its gaping maw, a horror, wrapped itself tightly around the man's thick neck, breaking it like a twig. I could hear the crunch and a final gasp for salvation as the blood spewed from his mouth. His body crumbled to the ground. I sat there, my body frozen to the snow, as I looked to the beast that would make me its next meal. Her body was colossal in comparison to mine.

Her eyes were a striking yellow, watching me for a slight move. She would be ready to pounce and leave me a ribboned mess.

'You lay atop my kin.' Like my mother's, the voice was deep and magical, blanketed over me with a soothing warmth. The birds flocked from atop their tree homes in a harmonious spree at the sound.

I tell you, my son. Odd as it may be, I heard the voice of a wolf. But trust me. Her voice was so similar to my first mother that it was unmistakable. It was like she had returned to me. So quickly. Although I know now that wasn't true.

'Remove yourself, child of man. My kin need not your vile body,' the wolf bellowed.

I looked down—what I had thought was the snow descending from the sky had been the bodies of pups. Except they were unmoving, their bodies held no beat. I didn't understand as I jolted, apologising, in fear of my life. I moved, I showed the pups to their mother.

With an ache, the wolf mother stepped silently over, her paws never plunging into the high-layered snow. She nestled her head into the pups, keeping it there for a long moment, her final goodbyes. I tore my eyes from them, to look at my mother's body, slowly being buried by the snow. I was struck with a petrifying sadness.

'The female human. Is that your kin?' the voice broke my frozen stance.

'Yes,' I spat out with a splatter of tears and snot. I have seen many dead since that moment, but for me then, the loss of my mother was overwhelming. In a moment of my own goodbye, I finally stepped over to my mother's corpse. I knelt. Then, I laid on my side, feeling the slick wet blood seep through my shirt and stick to my skin. I lifted my mother's arm, and for one last time, I put it around my shoulder before I nestled myself against her stiff frozen chest. My face warm with my own tears, I laid there, and prayed death would take me so I could reunite with my mother.

'You need not die this day, human boy.'

I lifted my head, and the wolf mother was still present. I thank that moment; I thank her for not leaving me.

'My mother and father both died. And I now have nowhere to go.'

'Boy, I will tell you now. If I could sacrifice my life so my kin could thrive, I would. But I no longer can. They have been slain and now lay away from my protection.' She burrowed down, placing her paws in front and laying her chin atop. 'Your mother made the ultimate sacrifice. Do not let it be in vain.'

As a child, I didn't understand why my mother left me. And I say this to you, my son, as a parent, it is something I would do now. And that is the ultimate sacrifice; dying for the one you love.

'Tell me your name, human boy?' the wolf asked.

'Ulf,' I said.

'My kin call me Chara,' she said.

'So, what would you have of me?' I asked.

'Live.'

It's funny. I remember this story so well, like it had only happened yesterday. I'll make a point, my son, to only tell you the important parts, or we would be here all night.

Sorry, anyway.

Time drifted, and the snow was melting into the blossoming brown earth. Leaves showed their withering self to us as they fell like rain. I felt the liquid muscles move beneath me as I laid snuggled deep within Chara's thick fur. I remember Chara always slept longer than me. She was a giant and ate a giant's meal in the morning and at night.

One morning, I rose early and found a sea of daffodils. My mother loved them, even now I remember as they sat atop our hearth. Every morning, my mother tended to the daffodils, cradling them against her nose and breathing their scent in. I wanted Chara to know of that memory and for her to love them. No, that is not true. I needed her to love them.

Every now and then, when I travelled with Chara, certain things would incite memory of my mother. Chara's protective nature guarded me, even though no threats were in sight. Her eyes would linger on me when I ventured too far from her presence. As a father now I understand, my son, for you do not know the threats that lurk, the sharp knife ready to strike you in the back.

That is correct; with her incredible vitality, Chara would jump into a river and catch plenty of fish, always leaving me to sit in awe as she moved like a dexterous cat.

'You have not made the fire yet?' she said, as she placed the fish atop the dry sticks.

'I am trying!' I will admit I was quick to temper as a child and failed at things a lot. I can create a significant fire now that rises higher than my own home. But that came with practice, and it started here.

'You need to place the stick in the groove,' Chara said as she pointed with her nose. 'And then, with the speed of a bird, spin the stick; it will create fierce friction, which will be your guide to an ember.'

My muscles grew tired, and I could feel them tighten, sweat dripping down my cheeks. Frustration was apparent as I felt my temper rise as the embers refused to spark. Chara just sat there, watching. Anger brewed as I heard a snicker from her. But I wouldn't surrender, not in front of her. Chara innocently moved forward, and I swear she lightly released a sigh, and there was a spark. I danced with happiness in tune with the flame.

'You dance well,' Chara said. Her paws were moving gently as if to hide it, but I know for certain on the gods above, she too had begun a dance of her own. 'We should now let the food cook so we can feast.'

I stopped my dance and looked at Chara, swallowing the sadness, feeling it fall to the bottom of my heart. At that moment, Chara released a warm smile. I felt my chest tighten, and I surrendered to the idea that she reminded me of my mother and your grandmother—in the form of a wolf.

This fire that rages in front of us. I taught you the same way, my son. Yes, that is where I began to learn how to care for myself. But funny, isn't it? I taught you something a wolf taught me.

With that memory deep in my mind, I collected the daffodils. I grabbed many, a whole basket's worth, to fill my small arms. I felt anticipation at the sight of Chara accepting them—

'Chara!' I bounded down like a bellowing boulder. Her body rose slowly from a restful slumber. Her once sharp, vicious eyes were now friendly and inviting, warmly accepting me.

'Boy, do not drift from me, perilous these lands are for a child,' she chided. She wasn't angry but spoke with authority, just like how my mother was with me when I did something wrong. But excitement fuelled my child's frame. I could almost jump for joy just in the hopes of her reaction.

'These are for you!' I swung my hands around to show her the efforts of my labour.

'Plants?' she asked me. She tilted her head to the side, her fluffy ears shot up in surprise.

'Daffodils! My mother's favourite,' I said, raising them higher.

'What am I to do with these, sweet boy?'

'You place your human nose to them and…smell!' I said, trying to raise them higher, almost pushing them into Chara's face. She leant forward, closing the gap, and I could hear the slow drift of air as she drank in the smell of the daffodils.

'So?' I asked. I felt my legs moving, excitement bellowing inside my body.

Chara licked her lips, her nose taking every bit of the scent in. 'It smells sweet, like honey,' she said. Sitting back, allowing her hind legs to support her, she almost became as tall as a tree, leaving me to stand in her shadow.

'It does? It does?' I asked.

'Child, have you not smelt a daffodil before?' she said.

'I have, its just, been so long since I have,' I said.

'Then please, my sweet, you too must smell the daffodil again,' Chara said.

So I placed the daffodils to my nose, and inhaled the sweet scent.

'What is the matter, my sweet?' I felt a tear run down my cheek because all I thought at that moment was:

'It smells like my mother.' I answered. It felt like she was close again, and I clutched the daffodils to my chest.

Take this daffodil, my son. Consume its aroma and understand what it was like to nestle your head in the warmth of your grandmother. Know her warmth, scent, and protection. I hope I have replicated it, like Chara did for me.

Chara and I had spent much time together, and the seasons moved along with the drifting wind. A bright sun rested high against the blue sky.

Thoughts of my mother weighed heavily on my mind. The breath taken from her, the knowledge that I had walked on from the grave I had left her in. I had learned to conjure fire, and not from her but from another. It stung, like the summer heat, it blistered my heart. I felt terrible as I looked at Chara, her strong and confident eyes, a reassurance that helped me.

'Your eyes cling to the ground, young Ulf,' Chara said.

'Leaving my mother where we did, was that okay?'

'Your mother's body feeds the earth now, young kin.' She stopped and turned to face me. Tilting her head, Chara's ears slanted down, covering the threatening sun. 'Your mother watches even now, proud to have graced you with the chance to grow with grey enriching your hair. Do not break with sadness and memories of her death.' She turned again and continued her walk. The warmth of the sun cloaked me this time. It felt like a release to talk.

Chara helped me more than I knew when I was a child. And my son, if sadness ever boils at the bottom of your heart, allow yourself to rely on those around you, for it is worth it. Trust me.

We continued the walk, and soon, the warm sun dissipated, and rain showered us. My clothes clung to me, and my only respite from the moist weather was when I clung to Chara.

'Dangers lurk behind every tree, sweet boy. Cling to me, I cannot smell well in this constant rain.'

When I was young, my body grew tired quickly, so we would rest and watch how this world behaved. Specifically, we saw battles between Vikings and Anglo-Saxons from afar. We would hear men's cries as their blades shattered against hard shields. Mother never would have allowed me at a young age to be that close to a battle, but Chara was different, always teaching me. She showed me how common death was and how easy it was to destroy one another.

My excitement kept Chara close to the battles, and when these battles ended and the winning lords took their men and left, looters would spawn. Foolishly, I strayed too close to one, and that was when I locked eyes with a looter. He sneered at me, baring his black teeth. I ran fast to find Chara, who was resting under a tree. I arrived at her side, panting.

'You left my side; what did I say? It is dangerous out there.' Chara said.

My stupid child mind was in fear of troubling Chara. I thought I had run far and fast enough that surely that looter couldn't have followed me. But oh, how foolish I was.

'Yes, Chara, I am sorry. I was watching another battle,' I finally responded. My eyes swayed to the side, unable to meet hers.

The following day, my happiness with Chara began to end as a gang of disgustingly vile looters stood around us and that one with the black teeth leered at me. He had followed me.

'A pup and a boy. Now, now, that ain't right,' one looter said.

'Boy? You see him? He is dirtier than the bog. Not a boy but another dirty pup to gut,' another looter said.

I could feel the heat stream out of Chara. Her response was a loud, thundering roar. And you could see the fear begin to claw its way around the looters. I saw them, and the way they looked at Chara. They feared her; she was a mighty wolf, larger than a tree, stronger than a bear. Her body enlarged, and she stood over me. She released a second thundering roar, but I heard what she said:

'No one touches my kin, for I will tear meat from bone for whoever dares!' Foolishly, the men didn't understand, and one long-haired man with a forester's axe ran towards Chara. Her body sprung like an arrow released from a bow, and she tore head from shoulder. Another ran for her. They had all silently agreed to target her as the immediate threat. I became like a crop in the middle of a field, planted in the dirt. I couldn't help Chara. As I saw a dagger scrape her side, I released a frightening scream. It reminded me of my mother when I, too, stood still, rooted and watching as a sword plunged into her chest.

From my scream, one man turned to me with his horrid smile. That would be his last smile as Chara's jaw wrapped around one of his ankles and threw him into a tree. I remember clearly the sounds of his bones crunching under the weight of pressure as his body collided with the tree.

'This wolf has the devil inside,' one of the last raiders said.

'Spawned from the war, we must slay it! It is an ill omen!'

'No!' I screamed. 'Not again!'

My mothers falling body slamming into the snow was deep in my mind. My tiny body ran for a fallen sword. I raised it to a raider and pointed it at him.

'The beast has taken the mind of the boy. We kill *it*, too.' The raider screamed.

A roar again, and Chara was on the man who spoke. Her claws grazed his chest, blood enriching the mud around him and me. But I watched as the final raider, turning from me, ran at Chara and plunged his axe into her side. An agonising scream left Chara as she turned, and with a final gasp from the man, Chara's teeth sunk into his shoulder, and she pulled him apart.

Chara's grey fur mixed with the rain, mud, and blood. She limped towards me before settling down. 'Are you well, my kin?' Her question left my heart in agony, as the axe was still deep within her side. I dropped the sword from my hand, a sword I couldn't swing.

'I must take the axe out,' I ran to her side, pulling it out. A light whimper this time. No loud roar to echo against the rain.

'Please, Mother, please,' were the only words that left me. To lose another mother; I knew it would break me. 'We must be away from the road, sweet child,' she said in a breaking voice. Despite her size and weakness, she leant on me, perhaps not as much as I wanted.

It didn't take long to find a small cave on the side of a large mountainside. Her body crumbled down, and the only noise we heard was the sound of rain as it crashed in front of the cave entrance. We could smell the night air as the sun dropped behind the tree line. I got close to her, knelt, laid down on my side, placed her paw around my shoulder and nestled deep into her chest. I kept my ear close, ensuring I could still hear her heartbeat. And a thought came to my mind: *I will find a way to protect.*

'Are you awake, sweet child?'

I rose quickly, my body still wet, the sun's glare beaming into my morning eyes.

'Chara!' I said, wrapping my hands around her furry neck.

'My kin, a scratch and an axe would never be my downfall, and you need not worry about that.' She reached her head back to where the axe had plunged into her, and she scraped her tongue along the scar. I collapsed into her, burrowing my face into her musty hide.

'I am glad,' I said.

'But, my kin, I am afraid that this will not end. There will be more. And with your child's body, an axe would surely leave you feeding the worms.' Her eyes were filled with sorrow.

'Then I shall learn to fight so I can one day protect you!' I said.

'I can only teach you how to fight like a wolf, my dear kin,' Chara said.

'Then I'll fight for you as a wolf,' I said. But she didn't respond, just let herself relax against the warm, protective sun.

'A human boy,' she said, slowly raising her aged body, 'can not learn how to fight as a wolf.'

'Chara!' But I broke down. Her eyes swelled, glistening with painful tears.

'I wish for your protection, young human boy,' Chara said.

'Then if not a wolf…I'll find another way so you can rely on me instead…'

'You do that then, but for now, let us rest.' A fiery heat raged within me. I thought of Mother that night, and how her body lay creasing the snow below her in a puddle of her own blood. *Never again,* my eyes ran across the scars that painted Chara's body.

'Never again will I lose another,' I whispered.

With my plan thick in my mind, Chara and I moved with the grace of a brown hare. We dodged the main road, keeping to the wooded thicket. The city of York sat dense against the falling sun.

We sat watching the city of York— the distant people living together, human with human, protecting

45

each other. I felt my heart shudder as it decided, and then Chara's paws landed heavily on the ground next to me. She slumped down, her large nose nestled into the corner of my neck—a warmth I miss dearly and have not felt since.

'What is it, child?' she asked.

'Chara, I need to go,' I said.

'What do you mean?'

'I need to leave to protect you,' I said, my eyes running along the sea of daffodils sprouting from the wet dirt around us. We were in a sea of them. It was a fitting place to leave her.

'You plan to return to your human folk?' Chara said.

'I do, Chara.'

Her cheek pushed into mine, and I could feel her scratchy fur gently tickling my skin. I felt the tug of my lips curling into a smile as the stream of tears began. I jerked away violently, pulling against myself and my childish need to be attached to her hip.

'It will be okay, Chara! I promise I will find you. I promise! And when I do, I will protect you from all evil.'

'I do not want you to leave, but if this is what you need, then I understand. I will let you go,' Chara said.

I was surprised and disappointed. Her response felt so easy, so earnest.

'You will let me go? So easily?' I asked. I felt like even though I had demanded to leave, she was abandoning me.

'I am a wolf, a creature of the woods. Your needs as a human are different from mine. I am sorry, dear. My heart shreds at the idea of losing another kin. But this is what you need. I know this, my sweet, my Ulf.'

Her words stung but invigorated me. I fought through the pit in my stomach. At the time, I didn't understand, but walking away taught me much, like standing on my own two feet.

I finally spoke, one last time, 'But I will find you when I am big and strong.'

She nodded silently, turned and limped away. I stood there and listened to her paws lightly rustle against the daffodils.

'I will find you, Chara! And when I do, I will be your protector.'

'Father, thank you for telling me about Chara.'

'I thought here, on the night Chara drew her final breath, you should hear our story.'

Ulf smiles at his son, who has his cheek pressed to the warm mane of a child of Chara. The smoke from the pyre reaches high and licks the clouds.

Ulf looks up and watches the smoke.

'Goodbye, Chara.'

At Your Beck and Call

Penny Foster

From the very moment my veil was lifted from my face, I was steadfast in the knowledge that my husband would be the eventual death of me.

England, Tower of London – 1557, January 17th

The winter wind picks up and howls through the towers surrounding the courtyard, making a shiver wrack across the mass of bodies that face me in their plush seats and winter coats. Their eyes watch as I shiver along with them with no coat to speak of. My coat is laid over the shoulders of the queen to be, once one of my ladies in waiting. I swallow back the familiar feeling of dread, a fiend that sits heavy in my stomach as I catch the joyful eyes of my husband, who laughs happily alongside his pregnant bride. My skin prickles again as I watch him lean in closer and whisper something to her. It appears his words are sweet or even suggestive and she giggles and nods as a chill runs up my spine, not from icy winds, or lack of furred coat, but from a memory.

1555, March 10th – England, Whitehall Palace. The Royal Wedding day.

The weight of the crown sat heavy upon my head, but the guilt and grief of wearing it and matching with a devil of a man instead of my betrothed, weighed more.

His voice was loud and foreign as he drank and danced merrily with the new members of court that had followed him from his home country. He had claim to the throne, rightly so, but he now had no competition as those in line before him now lay under layers of stone and dirt. He wore the blood of his fallen family proudly upon his hands. My betrothed having been his cousin, young, healthy, and in line for the throne, made him one of his first targets. But the monster saw no reason to change my wedding date, only the intended groom, remarking that every king needs a queen. The sudden grip of a meaty hand had squeezed my shoulder as its thick rings dug into my skin, dirty nails clawing into my dress.

'You sit like stale curd; you shall be fed to the dogs as such.' His words rolled down through my body and back up in a trembling shudder much like an emetic. As if to stop any bile from rising, his hand found purchase around my throat.

I swallowed against his hand and stared out to the dancing and feasting crowds, willing to keep my head high even as his breath fanned my shoulder again.

'Join your court in merriment, lest you conspire to enact heresy against the King?'

I shook my head and he led me from my seat into the hoard of dancing court members and their wives, all unknown faces he had brought from his home country.

Placating him was easy enough; a few dances, serving him goblets of wine or mead, and he had all but forgotten me as he recounted his battles and recent hunting successes to the members of his court. Sneaking away was just as easy amongst the crowd; even my heavy bridal gown of five-too-many layers caused no issue. I slipped out the balcony door and embraced the frigid wind of a stubborn winter that refused to let spring bloom.

'*Reine Catherine?*' The voice was soft and questioning as the thick accent rolled my name into one that could be a new name on its own. My eyes found him at the doors of the balcony. He seemed hesitant to approach. I sighed out a frosted puff of air and returned to looking out over the still-icy gardens.

'You may approach.' My words came out much sterner and more orderly than I intended, but I brushed the feeling off for he spoke the truth; I was now queen and thus should speak as one. He approached and stood beside me at a polite distance, his frosted breath coming into view from the corner of my eye as he spoke.

'You are not enjoying the celebrations?' he asked. My eyes moved to him as I judged just how candidly I could speak.

'You are of this court, yes?'

'*Oui, ma reine –*' He quickly cleared his throat and spoke again the same words but in a different shape, 'Yes, my queen.'

'You think me a fool to not know simple French?' I asked and glanced at him, watching his eyes widen before he dropped to one knee with his hand over his heart.

'Forgiveness, Your Majesty. I mean not to offend.' He bowed his head and held his position faithfully until I called him up.

'You require no such thing.' I smiled at him as he rose up, visibly relieved. 'And what might your name be?' I inquired. He gave a sweeping bow, plucking the brimmed feathered cap from his head once more before speaking in his bent pose.

'*Monsieur Hervé Beaumont III* at your beck and call, *ma reine*,' he announced.

'I do believe I will make you a man of your word, *Monsieur Beaumont*.'

By morning's first light the frost had cleared, and spring had begun to blossom.

1555, May 23rd   Hampton Court. Queen Catherine's first spring.

Spring is a time for rebirth and growth, but within the castle it was for anger and piecing glares, as no growth called my womb home.

The king had made peace with the surrounding royals of furthering lands, having strong-armed them all into submission. His keenness to continue his blessed bloodline only grew the longer he lurked around the castle, his bloodlust turned to a fidgeting need to further cement his claim on the kingdom. But nothing came, and his response was vitriol.

I stood at the chamber door after having seen the physicians out, grasping my hands tightly together as I willed myself still while his thundering voice cursed in his mother tongue. Vases cast to the floor and shattered before he stomped over the heaped flowers to me. My breath caught in my throat as his dark eyes met mine, his fists clenched white.

'Are you barren? Did you know upon our marriage?' His words were steady but deep with rage as he glowered down. I opened my mouth to speak but his hand found my shoulder first, his thick digits pressing into my flesh as he sneered his words. 'Lie to me, wench, and it shall be your final breath.'

'Forgiveness, my husband.' My words were a trembling whisper. 'These things take time,' a gasp was forced from my lips as his grip tightened before I scrambled to finish my thought, 'but may God see time and I fit soon!'

He was still for several heartbeats, I counted ten as it raced in my ears before he dropped his hand and returned to the table and chair that held his goblet of wine. He downed it before addressing me.

'Pray He does. Begone.' I took no further instruction as I fled out the chambers and walked curtly down the hall, my body urging me to run, but the eyes of the foreign maids who made no effort to hide their eavesdropping kept me proper and ladylike. I found solace in a darkened corner under the thick suffocating curtains, my palms flying to my eyes as if to physically hold my tears at bay. Yet the tears did not obey me, streaking my powdered cheeks to fall upon my dress and leave white blotches.

I stayed hidden as the sun began to lower, only being roused from my spot when a familiar accented voice called to me.

'*Ma raine?*' I frantically wiped my cheeks as Monsieur Beaumont crept to the curtain's edge and revealed me. Despite my attempts, it was clear from the look in his eyes that I looked unsightly, but instead of a sneer of disgust he joined me beneath the curtain. It was highly inappropriate and yet I did not care in that moment, craving even an ounce of the warmth and softness I had been depraved thus far. He held me gently and spoke in whispers that tickled my ear. 'Blessed jewels and holy prayers take time.'

He held me until the sun dipped down and I was called for dinner.

1555, June 12th Hampton Court. Queen Catherine's first summer.

Summer often meant festivals, dances, and hunting trips. Whether hosting garishly large feasts or procuring the meats for one, the king and his court never passed up the opportunity to display wealth and ability.

I sat and watched the tall bushes and trees of the garden sway in the warm breeze before returning to my stitching work, a crease pinching my brows as I pondered over the scandalised whispers the maids and ladies in waiting prattled.

'Fine afternoon, Your Majesty.' His voice rang like a bell but was never jolting or jarring as he came to stand beside me, his eyes training over my needle work before finding the frown in my brow.

'Something troubles you?' I nodded and let my fingers still while looking up at him.

'Be true and speak only such to me, *Monsieur Beaumont*,' my voice wavered like a jolted goblet, threatening to spill and tip before I forced myself steady, 'Have I fallen out of the king's favour? I heard the whispers His Majesty has taken a lady of mine as his mistress.'

My question seemed to shock him as he took a moment to collect himself before resting on one knee and bowing his head.

'Even the king would be a fool to lack favour for you, *ma reine*.'

'A fool, you say?' I question and catch the slight tremor in his shoulders as he understood what his words could imply. But instead of retreating, he hardened them with a certainty that must have been as strong as steel.

'*Oui*. Only a fool would willingly throw himself from your arms in favour of another. Our king is a gloriously lucky man to have you at his side. He should know this.' His words, while not a shout, screamed of his loyalties. Slowly he raised his head and watched me with eyes of emeralds that seemed to glint in the sun. I leaned in close, blocking the sun from his eyes and returning them to their deep comforting forest green as I held myself a sliver away from him. My voice was low as I whispered to him in an almost playful tone.

'You mean to enact heresy against our God-like-king?' I tilted my head slightly and watched his eyes for a flicker of fear or a twitch of doubt, but nothing came, only the relaxing and lowering of his gaze to my lips as he replied.

'At your beck and call, *ma reine.*'

1557, January 17th England, Tower of London. Queen Catherine's execution.

My eyes snap to the king's rising form as he quiets the crowd with a single raising of his hand, large and covered in jewelled rings that catch the light as the clouds shift over the sun. I find my own and twist it around on my thumb. It helps steel my nerves.

'Queen Catherine of England, you have been accused of adultery and heresy to your king. You have failed to produce an heir and...' My eyes lower along with my head as I stroke over the dainty ring of gold and emerald that lay around my thumb, while my mind wonders away from the lengthy list of my crimes, some fair and just while the rest schemed up to seal my fate. The light catches the edges of the gem and only makes my heart ache more as I remember Hervé's eyes that day.

1556, November 2nd Whitehall Palace. Queen Catherine's second autumn.

Hervé and I had wondered around the decaying gardens of golden and orange hues while our hands secretly brushed beneath our coats. We walked out of sight of the looming castle or peering eyes with the only sound between us being the crunching of leaves as we ventured through the topiaries.

Finally, as we rounded the last hedge, his warmth found my hand and pulled it to his cool lips, refusing to part from it even as he spoke.

'The king is set to travel this afternoon along with the entire court for several days, *ma reine.*' His words a slight mumble, as though what he was saying wasn't important and only an obstacle to him enjoying my warm hands.

'I am taken aback you did not join them,' I softly pressed my knuckle under his chin and used it to raise his eyes to mine, 'I do know how you enjoy a good hunt.' He chuckled softly before speaking, grasping my hand and lowering it.

'If you are surprised that I would prefer to stay in your company, then I must make clear my intentions for you,' something cold and thin slid onto my thumb before he graced my hand with another grinning kiss. *'ma reine.'*

I pulled back my hand and inspected the thin golden band that glinted and shone in the autumn sun, a fine piece with an even finer gem of emerald. He smiled and gently corralled me into the shadow of the hedge and excitedly showed me how the stone changed hues in the shade compared to the light, though my eyes were on something I desired far more. My hands found his cheeks as I stepped closer, turning us and pressing him into the greenery as I leant in.

'I shall carry it always, so you are forever with me.' I whispered and closed the gap between our lips as his hands encircled my waist.

1557, January 7th – Greenwich palace. Queen Catherine's second winter.

Morning approached in misty blue blankets of light as the early winter sun struggled to rise and warm the world. But the cold did not touch me nor him as we lay resting in the royal chambers.

Hidden inside the darkness and shielded by the bed's thick velvet curtains, my fingers stroked through Hervé's hair. He laid still and content in my arms, his eyes fluttering every few moments before he opened them truly and stared into my own.

'Words linger on your tongue. Speak, my love.' I whispered as I continued smoothing back his hair. He sighed and tightened his arm around me.

'The angels have yet to welcome me, but I am sure I have died.' He whispered back as his hand captured mine from his hair and kissed it tenderly.

'I forbid you to speak of such things,' I demanded, nuzzling my way under his chin. My lips finding his neck as I mumbled against his throat. 'I would not know what to do if you left my side.'

He hummed deep in his throat as his hand rubbed along my back.

'I will not deny the joy I would feel if you were to cry for me, mourn for my loss as if I was precious—'

'You *are* precious to me. Irreplaceable.' I interrupted and squeezed him close as if he were to disappear from my grasp in that very moment. He laughed and continued to rub my back.

'Do not fear, *ma reine*. I mean to go nowhere without you, and if I am to leave,' his fingers freed his neck from my lips as his tilted my head up and leaned in closer until his lips were a hair away from my own. 'I should take you with me.' His lips finally touched mine as his words touched my heart, making it flutter as he held me and poured his love into our kiss.

The sound of the chamber door slamming open caused us to jump. I left his arms and tried to intercept before the bed's curtains were yanked open, but my hand barely touched the fabric as it was ripped away to reveal us to the king. He stood there, tall and looming, with a face the colour of rubies, eyes so tight and glared that you could not see the colour of them. My mouth opened to speak any excuse I could muster, but the stinging sharpness as one of his rings caught my cheek killed all the words on my tongue. Hervé's arms found me and pulled me back as the king dropped the curtain and pursued his guards, leaving us in the darkness of our once-peaceful moment.

1557, January 16th – Tower of London. One day until Queen Catherine's execution.

My hands found the thick metal bars as I pressed my body against the stone wall, tears streaming down my face as my body heaved and wracked with sobs. It was hard to see through the tears and made more so with the height of the tower, but I could still see Hervé as he was dragged out before the court in rags and forced to kneel.

He was read his list of crimes but neither of us listened as his eyes looked up and found me, his chained hands reaching up to his lips as he blew a kiss my way before the hooded man grabbed him and pulled him towards the gallows. I screamed and sobbed, pushing my arm through the bars and reached out for him desperately; I was sure all below could hear me. I screamed for him as the rope was laced around his neck as his final words rung in my ears before he was ripped away from my arms that morning.

'Do not watch, *ma reine*. Shut your eyes and hold your ring close.' I ripped away from the small window and held his ring to my lips, chanting and whispering prayers to a higher god that pain would not keep him, that angels would welcome him, that he could forever escape damnation at the hands of a king that thought himself a God.

I stayed kneeling on the dirt-filled cracks of the tower floor, lips sealed to his ring long after morning melted into the afternoon and then night. The sobbing never stopping even as my voice was lost to screaming his name and pleading to any divine being that would listen; to meet him again, to have him in my arms once more, I wagered any price. But morning came and he did not.

1557, January 17th – Tower of London. Queen Catherine's execution.

The ropes swing in the wind as it howls once more the cry of a mournful wolf. A single too-wide gap remains on the gallows, as they had yet to replace the rope from the morning prior.

The sound of thudding footsteps makes me cast my eyes in wonder. Would it be the same man as yesterday morning? Is he now tasked to wield a sword and not rope? My mind races with thoughts as the icy air grips and grows thorns in my lungs with each quick breath. My eyes find the king's as he sit waiting, watching with keen interest as the wooden block is brought before me. I can feel the racing of my heart, a wild animal in my chest as fear consumes me. The sound of distant stone grinding is surely the sharpening blade that would meet my neck. I grip the skirts of my dress as tears sting my eyes, hands clasped in front to feign the properness or calmness I was taught to retain as queen. I do not want to die. My hands grip tighter before I feel my ring pressing into my palm. The fingers of my other hand caress it softly as I trace the jewel it holds, the thoughts slowing as I rub my fingers along its smooth surface.

The grinding stops and so do my tears, my heart slowing in my chest as I pet and stroke along the cool gem and metal while I wait. The sting of my lungs remains as I kneel down and rest my body upon the block, shutting my eyes as I press my ring up into my chest so he would be close to my heart. We will meet again soon. The sound of shifting clothes and a soft swoosh pulls a frighten gasp from me.

I hope he's waiting for me.

Lost at Sea

Jesse Allan

Port Royal, Jamaica – 1706

One day. That is all the time that has passed on this tiny island. To Cal, it feels like centuries—eons—since he washed up on the beach of Port Royal. Frozen, exhausted, afraid. Yesterday, he was an Irishman on his way to The New World with his sister. Now, he is a desperate man eliciting the help of his friend-turned-pirate to find his missing sibling.

'Perhaps you can come with me?'

Adam's words pull Cal back to the moment. He turns his attention away from the wrecked boat on the other side of the dock—a tragedy that occurred sometime after he was tossed overboard—back to the man in front of him. Cal sizes up his old friend, taller by three inches and twice as broad since they last spoke. Adam looks back expectantly.

'How would that help me?' Cal replies, brow furrowed.

Adam crosses his arms, 'Well, my Captain has asked me to take a solo trip to Cape Cod to sell some goods and collect some mail. Cape Cod happens to be where many pirates take their surviving hostages, so, if Alexandria is alive it's possible we'll run into her there.' He combines 'it's' and 'possible' into one word; another thing about him that's changed since he left home.

Cal bites the inside of his cheek, considering Adam's proposition. The thought of being over water again turns his stomach, as does the thought of being in a boat manned by one person. 'What happens if we are attacked?'

Adam shrugs off Cal's concern, 'Ah, won't happen. Trust me, pirates don't attack other pirates. But even so, I know I don't look like much now but trust me I can hold my own.' He flexes and laughs.

Cal laughs along with him, looking away when he feels the heat rising in his face. Adam is mostly muscle, always was from working on his family's farm. He fits right into this island, full of heavy boats and anchors and things to be pushed and pulled.

Cal clears his throat, 'But, could I hold my own? Say, if the water turns treacherous?'

'I can teach you the basics of sailing,' Adam offers, 'we'll be isolated on the ocean, after all, with little else to do.'

Cal nods at the ground, scrunching his face. He turns his attention to the boat, 'So, this is yours?' he asks. The small vessel bobs over the gentle waves lapping at the dock.

'Well, no, this here is part of the captain's fleet, but I've sailed this and boats like this many times.' Adam leans on a wooden pole holding up the dock and slaps the side of the boat, causing it to bob a little faster, 'Now, this here is a sloop. Not the fanciest, nor the biggest, but it cuts through the waves nicely,' he emphasises 'cuts' by shooting his hand out through the air, 'and, it's small enough for one man to manage on his own.'

Cal nods slowly, exaggerating the movement, inserting small 'mm's' and 'ah's' where he deems appropriate.

Adam continues, 'Not to worry, though, our journey to Cape Cod is through smooth waters. We won't need to strategically weave through anything.' He mumbles something like 'I hope' under his breath. Cal doesn't comment on it.

'Alright,' Cal looks back to Adam, 'when do you leave?'

'Right now, if you're so willing.' Adam smiles and sweeps an arm towards the boat.

Cal hesitates, aware of the dryness in his mouth, and the rushing waters of his mind. The memories from last night—pirates shouting, children crying, his sister ripped from his side—linger in his mind's eye. The shivers shooting down his spine freeze him firmly in place. He considers telling Adam how he's presently feeling, but the thought of being vulnerable doesn't appeal to the side of him that's forever influenced by society's image of manhood.

Cal looks to Adam, and that seems to be enough to communicate all he's feeling. Adam's expression softens, 'If it's too soon, I understand.'

Cal firmly shakes his head, 'If Alexandria is alive, I have to find her as soon as possible. I will be okay,' he nods along to his own words, 'I trust you, Adam.'

With that, Cal carefully climbs aboard the sloop. Adam swings on after him.

Once aboard, Adam begins fiddling with the ropes and sail; Cal watches him work. His swift and automatic movements seem to suggest years of prior knowledge. 'How long ago did you leave that merchant ship?' Cal asks.

'Oh, uh, three, four years ago? I lasted a few months, then I learned how much more a pirate makes in a year. I decided this would be a better use of my time away, so I might return home with more for my family.' Adam speaks while tightening and slackening different ropes, not distracted by the switching between roles.

Seeing how expertly his friend moves calms Cal down some. 'Makes sense. And how do you find the work, as a pirate?'

'It's alright. I've learned how to use a sword, but thankfully, I haven't had to use it much. I'm more suited to the sailing and navigating.' Adam pushes off the dock and positions himself at the sail. 'Alright, off we go.'

Cal watches the dock recede. The further the boat sails from still land, the further the nausea creeps up his throat. His gaze drifts to the wrecked boat, bobbing in and out of view behind massive pirate ships. The boat he and his sister had travelled on, the boat that was attacked mere hours ago. His head spins, his mouth waters, his eyes prick.

'How're we feeling?' Adam calls out.

'Not superb,' Cal exhales a shivering breath.

Adam nods, 'Alright. How about I show you the ropes? Help take your mind off it?'

'Huh?' Cal enquires.

Adam smiles, 'I said, how about I teach you how to sail?'

'Oh, of course,' Cal huffs and shakes his head. 'You will have to teach me some of that pirate lingo, too.'

Cal carefully meanders over the baggage to reach where Adam stands. He uses a hand to steady himself on his friend's shoulder, noticing how tense Adam is, he assumes from guiding the sail.

Adam reaches back and grabs Cal's left hand, guiding it to the correct position on the rope. 'This hand here, and,' he reaches back and grabs Cal's right hand, guiding it to the opposite rope, 'this hand here.' Adam keeps his hands positioned over Cal's on the ropes. Cal is aware of how close their bodies are.

'Pull this to go left,' Adam guides Cal's left hand down and the boat veers left, 'and pull this to go right,' Adam pulls down Cal's other hand and the boat veers right. Adam corrects the path by pulling gently on Cal's left hand, returning them to their original position. 'There you go, try it yourself.'

Adam takes his hands off, hovering them a few inches above where Cal holds the ropes. He inhales, exhales, pulls slightly on the left rope. The boat leans gently, cutting through the water. He does the same with his right, watching the boat as it glides through the waves, as effortlessly as a bird flies through the air. Thinking of it like that—like he is flying above the ocean and not moving within it—helps him calm down.

'Not bad. If you continue progressing this well, we can sail in shifts.' Adam's gentle encouragement and warm laugh loosens the knot in Cal's chest. He relaxes, if only a little, at being in control of the boat carrying him, and watched over by the man he trusts.

But with the calming of his anxiety surfaces the grief of his lost sister. She is out there, somewhere. Stolen, lost, afraid.

The first day comes and goes, uneventfully. The pair dock at Charles Towne as the sun is setting, casting dramatic pink-red shadows over the seaside settlement.

Adam vaults over the side of the boat before it stops moving. He ties it down, then addresses Cal. 'Alright, wait here. I'm going to ask around and see if anyone has picked up mail for my Captain.'

Cal nods, and with that Adam disappears amongst the burly seamen. Cal marvels at how seamlessly Adam fits in with this crowd, as if he were built to be amongst them. Something Cal, with his lanky frame, cannot relate to.

As soon as Adam is gone Cal carefully climbs off the boat and onto the dock. He grimaces at the grimy ground—the green spots and the dark black colour of the wood—but despite his aversion to dirt he favours the still ground over the bobbing boat. He sits, paying no mind to the odd looks he receives.

Adam returns shortly, empty-handed. Cal looks up and smiles. 'Where do we sleep tonight?'

'Ah, you won't like this,' he nods down. 'On the boat.'

Cal follows his gesture. 'Uh, is there somehow a cabin under there?'

'No, what I mean to say is, we'll be sleeping on the deck.'

'Oh. Well, I don't know if I can sleep with the,' Cal waves his hands about, 'ocean bobbing us around.'

'Well, unless you have coin for an inn it's the boat or the dock you're sat on.'

Cal sighs. 'Boat it is, then. Do we maybe have coin for some ale?'

Adam shakes his head from side to side. ,'Well, perhaps—ah, hold on, I packed some rum here somewhere.'

Adam climbs back on the boat and begins rifling through the bags. From one bag he pulls a bottle full of clear liquid.

'What on Earth is *rum?* Cal asks, considering the transparent and unlabelled bottle.

'An alcohol distilled from sugar cane. Somewhat like an ale, but much more potent.' Adam opens the bottle, sniffs it, and offers it to Cal.

Cal climbs back aboard, gripping the sides of the hull at the slight sway of the boat. He takes the bottle from Adam's hand, sniffs the liquid, and recoils sharply at the stinging sensation it inspires in his nostrils.

Adam laughs, 'A lot more potent than ale. I admit, it might be too much.'

Cal shakes his head. 'No such thing.' He takes a swig and thrusts it back in Adam's direction as he turns and hacks over the side of the boat.

Adam laughs hard, weakly grabbing back the bottle. 'Oh, no, poor Cal.'

'Shut your bastard mouth,' Cal retorts, which only makes Adam laugh harder.

'Ah, I would, but it's nice finally seeing you taken down a peg.' Adam takes a smooth swig from the bottle. 'I intend to enjoy this rare moment while it lasts.'

Cal glares at him through watery eyes before breaking out into a smile that turns into a soft laugh. 'Okay, okay. That is fair.'

'It takes some getting used to, I admit,' Adam takes another swig and offers the bottle back to Cal. He takes it, drinking from it with conservative sips.

The pair lie back side-by-side on the boat. The sun has disappeared under the horizon, revealing in its wake a sea of stars.

Cal is drifting from his body. His spirit vibrating at the boundaries of his physical being.

He is nothing but an animal, existing in the world. An animal, stuck on one side of a cavernous drop, unsure how to reach the other side. To his right is a bridge, but the animal brain—too small and simplistic—cannot comprehend how the foreign architecture might connect him to where he wants to be. Then, along comes Adam, his saviour.

Cal looks to Adam with the same admiring gaze he uses to look at the stars. Here is a man gaining nothing from helping him, but doing it anyway, simply because he wants to help.

Cal's vision blurs the more he drinks. He doesn't mind, though; the more numb he is, the less he feels the roiling waves beneath him.

'What are you staring at?' Adam asks.

Cal refocuses his gaze, seeing Adam looking back at him, smiling wide. Cal giggles, drunk and unsure what to make of the aching feeling that warms his chest when he looks at his friend. He deflects with a joke, 'Aw, just your beautiful eyes, you handsome devil.' He laughs more, punching his friend's arm and looking back at the sky. He continues, 'No, really. Thank you for helping me. I wouldn't have known what to do without you.'

'Oh, of course, anything for a…friend.' Adam's tone is deflated. After a pause he continues, 'So, how do you find the ocean now?'

Cal contemplates his question, 'I am unsure. I must separate it, I think, from the ocean I was attacked on. But I tell you what,' he holds the bottle to his lips, 'this rum helps a great deal.'

Adam snickers, 'I thought it might. And this coast is much less aggressive than the open water between Europe and America.'

'This is true,' Cal agrees. 'And the pirate life, do you enjoy it?'

'I s'pose. Not my first choice, but the money I make'll be good for my family's farm. It hasn't been doing so well lately, and after my mother passed, it was like my father aged another ten years. My brothers are old enough now to help some, but what would really help is better equipment. I left to make that money.'

'Oh, right,' Cal looks at Adam; he is looking up at the sky, 'I have never thought of it like that.'

Adam looks back at him, his face sorrowful. 'You've never had to think about it.'

Cal looks at his friend, seeing the struggle—the internal battle he literally cannot afford to have—eating him alive. 'Why not stay and help on the farm?'

Adam shrugs, 'I needed to leave, eventually. Find people like me.' He trails off, looking sidelong before looking back to Cal. 'I got lonely, back in Ireland.'

'You, lonely?' Cal couldn't help but be a little offended that his long-time friend hadn't been fulfilled by his presence.

'As in, I had no one to relate to. Not like I do here, amongst these men.'

'What's different about them?'

'Well, some of them prefer men, too.'

'Oh.' Cal looked at Adam. He wasn't lying.

Adam continued. 'My family doesn't know. I don't know how, or if I should, tell them.'

'That is your choice, Adam.' Cal smiles at him, hoping it brings him comfort.

Adam returns the smile, 'I know. Thank you.'

The pair fall silent, unsure what else to say.

The salt in the air attacks Cal as he stirs from his sleep. It lays in a thick blanket over his skin, his hair. He licks his lips and tastes the salt, familiar and sickening, like the same meal eaten thrice a day for too many weeks.

He opens his eyes fully, shielding them against the beating sun. Adam is standing above him at the sail, pulling the ropes with more vigour than he did yesterday. 'Where are we now?' Cal asks groggily.

Adam looks back at him. 'Ah, finally! Good morning!'

The waves are choppier here than along the strip they sailed yesterday. Cal guesses, correctly, it is because of the higher winds. They beat at the sail, and as they do, Adam tenses and pulls and struggles— resisting the wind's commands. As he does so, Adam glances at the receding coastline. Cal realises he is trying to veer their boat left, so they might rest until the storm passes.

Cal supports himself on the lip of the hull, pulling himself into a seated position. The boat is flying further out of control. Like a child has stirred their spoon around the bowl of the ocean, and the vortex it creates is pulling them—

—down.

I shouldn't have set foot on this boat. I shouldn't have dragged Adam along with me.

Down.

It's my fault we're here. It's Alexandria all over again.

Down.

A vicious wind knocks Adam down. His head slams against the hull, his limp body falling to the deck.

With no one at the ropes the boat is tossed over the waves. At the mercy of the ocean. Vortex pulling them down.

'Adam!'

Cal grabs at Adam, the tears in his eyes falling to his face. Adam twitches. He's alive.

Through the whirlwind, Cal sees the ropes whipping about.

Cal shakes his head. Shakes his tears. He reaches for the whipping rope. He grabs it, holds it firm. Carefully, he pushes himself up through his legs, onto his feet. He stands at the sail, as he has watched Adam do. He grabs both ropes and he pulls—

The wind is dying back. Cal sails to the shore. The boat rams against the bay. Cal jumps down onto the sand and pulls the wooden body up the beach, far enough that the waves cannot pull it back.

The rain starts. Like tiny daggers pricking the skin. Cal glazes over the supplies and grabs Adam's limp body by the armpits, hoisting him onto the beach. Adam's head lolls uncomfortably, but his chest still lifts, letting Cal know he's still breathing. Adam is so, so much heavier than Cal anticipated. Nevertheless, he scans the cliffside for a hole, and his eyes land on a small one to his right. Trying not to be rough, he drags Adam up the beach and to the small shelter. He sits on the sand and pulls Adam up to his chest. They are at least safe from the wind and rain.

A heat builds in Cal's chest. A hand, squeezing his heart and lungs. The pressure warms behind his eyes and the tips of his ears. He is red; contrasted with the endless blue-grey outside. It releases out of him in shaking sobs. Silent, at first, then a quiet, shameful moaning.

How lucky we are, to have survived. How could anyone survive this?

'Cal…'

Through the stinging tears, Cal sees Adam looking up at him, bewildered. He sits up carefully, wincing and holding the back of his head. Their faces are inches apart in the tight space.

'I am sorry,' Cal struggles out between sobs.

Adam puts a hand on Cal's shoulder and moves it to his cheek. 'For what? You needn't be sorry, you didn't bring about the storm.'

'No, not for that,' Cal takes a deep breath. 'I am sorry for dragging you out here with me, on a pointless mission. Adam, she—'

Cal cuts himself off, unable to admit what he can no longer deny.

Adam pulls Cal to him. Pulls his head to his chest, rests his hand on the back of his head. Cal wraps his arms around Adam and tries not to sob.

'You're okay,' Adam whispers into his hair.

'She is gone, and it is my fault.' Admitting it aloud brings out something in Cal. Releases a tension he didn't know he was holding. A hope he didn't know he had. Like the dam holding back the lake has crumbled, and the pain is washing over him in unrestricted waves.

They sit like that for a while. Adam holding Cal as he shudders against his chest. The rain outside is relentless. In the distance there is thunder.

'What do I do now?' Cal asks once his sobbing has subsided enough to speak.

Adam strokes his hair, whispering close to his ear, 'You keep going. Keep living.'

'But how, knowing what I have done, do I keep going?'

Adam sighs, 'You just keep going anyway. This grief will pass. You'll live through it, trust me. Besides, it's not your fault.'

Cal sits up, 'How? I am the one that wanted to leave. Alexandria only accompanied me because she did not want me to travel alone,' he looks out to the ocean, 'and look where that landed her.'

'She chose to leave, same as you did. She might have been influenced by your decision, but she still made a choice. You cannot blame yourself forever.'

'No, that is not true! She only left because I was leaving! Because…'

Adam looks at Cal though lowered brows, 'Because what?'

Cal looks Adam in the eyes. 'Because my parents disowned me. After they found me with a man.'

Adam's eyes widen, whispering a single 'oh,' so quiet it's almost unintelligible.

Cal's bottom lip quivers. 'And now you know.'

The rain beats like a drum against the cliff. Inside, the pair are silent.

Cal cannot look Adam in the eye. Despite what his friend admitted to him last night, he still feels shame washing over him.

Adam doesn't say anything in response. Instead, he pulls Cal in again, wrapping his arms tight around him. 'You're safe here.'

Cal didn't realise how much he needed to hear it until now. He wraps his arms back around Adam.

Eventually, Adam pulls away. Cal does the same. They sit facing each other again, inches apart.

'The crew I'm with, none of them care about preferences. So long as you contribute your share of work. You're welcome to stay with us, for as long as you like.'

Cal smiles, 'I'd be delighted.'

'Maybe I can teach you more than sailing,' Adam says, smiling.

'Oh? What do you mean by that?' Cal raises his brow.

'Navigation. Maybe a bit of sword work. Why, what did you think I meant?'

Cal laughs, 'Nothing, nothing.' He puts his hand over Adam's where it rests on the rock.

They wait for the storm to pass together.

Better the Demon you Know

Rachel Bauer

London – 1870

Ava was completely off her head. Being the assistant of the spiritual swindler Madam Owens had all but confirmed there was nothing on the other side. And yet…

The demon she had summoned waved away incense smoke, looking either bored or inconvenienced. However, they didn't have animal parts or extra heads as Ava had expected of a demon—they looked like a regular man in his late twenties: black vest under navy green coat, beige trousers, cravat, and gloves, but no top hat on their styled brown hair. If they hadn't just appeared before her, she would've thought they'd walked in from the street.

Regaining her senses, she remembered the first step from the grimoire.

Identify the daemon before thee. The one summoned may not be what thou seeketh.

Chin up, she spoke, 'Are you known as Vual? Answer me truthfully.'

'No.' The demon was barely paying attention, their eyes wandering around the drawing room, taking in the sheer red curtains colouring the light of the sinking sun; the tarot cards, planchette and paper on the circular table surrounded by chairs; the crowded bookshelves. They then turned their eyes to the young woman before them: thin, bruised, and soot-stained, clothed in an old Regency dress which was rather unflatteringly shapeless and plain, the recent fashion trends considered.

'Dantalion? Forneus? Raum? Bo-?'

'I'm going to stop you there. My name is Charlemagne.'

'That is none of the seventy-two demons.'

'I'm surprised you bothered to memorise them. Look, let's just get on with whatever you're after. We don't need all...this.' They gestured vaguely.

Ava belatedly remembered the warnings from the grimoire.

The daemon will trick thee. Assert authority upon the hellspawn.

Inhaling sharply, she spoke, 'Behold your punishment if you be disobedient. Behold—'

Charlemagne ignored her. 'Let me guess; you are an assistant to a medium. They find you abhorrent but probably keep you around because you're still small enough to clean the chimney flue for free. You decided to summon a demon for whatever *unoriginally selfish* reason you're about to tell me, using one of their questionably authentic spellbooks, and somehow managed it.'

Ava baulked at the cutting words. Truthfully, she had only done this on a whim, emboldened by Madam Owens' absence. But now that it had indeed worked, she had to follow procedure for her own safety. It was time for the second step; binding the demon.

'Welcome, spirit Charlemagne. I say—'

'Skip that bit. Just say the end.'

Ava, used to holding her tongue, pinched her lips at yet another interruption. 'I bind you to remain affably and visibly here for as so long as I require you, and not to depart without my licence until you have faithfully and truly performed my will without any falsity.'

'I, Charlemagne, do swear, promise and pledge to you in the presence and before the Great Lord.'

'And the rest of it. *If you please.*' This was the one thing she could not, would not, do carelessly.

Charlemagne lifted their top lip in annoyance, revealing a neat row of sharp triangular teeth, and Ava thought they might not continue. But thankfully, they did. 'I bind myself to you, at all times and places, until your life's end. Let the powers of Heaven witness that I have hereto pledged my hand to you. Amen. There. Happy?'

They had still heavily paraphrased it, but when the demon's amulet pinned on Ava's waist flashed, she was satisfied that the contract had been made. Ava nodded.

'Right. What would you have me do, *Master*?'

Ava puffed herself up. 'I should like to go to a ball.' Madam Owens always insisted that a proper lady needed an escort to leave the house, and here one had finally appeared.

Charlemagne studied her flatly. 'I can see why you'd need a demon's help.'

'Would you *kindly* stop interrupting me? I have a stipulation; I must return before midnight.' Beyond the red curtains, the sunlight was already beginning to pale.

'You're really committed to being Cinderella, aren't you?'

'It is merely a coincidence. Madam Owens will return at that hour.'

Charlemagne nodded slowly, one eyebrow raised and eyes slightly squinted. 'And that's a problem because...?'

'It is in poor taste to discuss such things.' Ava's tone was clipped, defensive.

'Right. I'm not that interested anyway. Well then, your wish is my command.' Despite their tired tone, Charlemagne bowed like a gentleman. When they rose, they snapped their fingers, bringing to their hands a bundle of clothes and accessories. Ava's eyes widened, but before her protest emerged from her open mouth, the bundle was thrown at her, and she lurched forward to catch it. But with another snap, she found the old Regency dress in her gloved hands instead. The ballgown and boots had seemingly been modified to fit on her smaller frame.

At Ava's speechless stare, Charlemagne shrugged. 'It's faster this way. And I'm sure you'd want to maintain *proper decorum.*'

'I cannot wear these things! These are all Madam Owens' belongings!'

'Why not? It's not like I can pull a dress from thin air. And all of yours are...ugly.'

Ava's lips pursed. After all, she was already disobeying the Madam by leaving the house. And summoning a demon in the drawing room.

'What she doesn't know won't hurt her,' Charlemagne pushed in a sing-song voice.

'Still...'

Charlemagne rolled their eyes. 'How about you just take a look?' Another snap of the fingers brought the Madam's short standing mirror before them.

Ava crept towards it, not used to the sheer weight of the gown, and a bit hesitant, too.

Bruises and soot stains marred her skin no longer. She was wearing an off-the-shoulder pale blue ballgown with rows of artificial flowers on the back of the overskirt and lace along the hems, a pink rose adorning her chest below a pendant necklace, and her brown hair, tied with a flowering headpiece, fell in tight ringlets.

The demon was silent as tears of complicated emotion welled in Ava's eyes, and then as she composed herself.

'Let us depart,' she announced.

The brilliant orange-red band on the horizon, the last evidence of the day's sun, quickly shifted into purple and pink overhead.

'Isn't it gorgeous?' Ava said. She had once overheard from a foreign client, in his accented and clumsy English, that only the London area had such vibrant and unique sunset colours. Ava had taken a bit of unearned pride in that, even if it may have been false flattery.

Charlemagne tilted their head in acknowledgement. 'Indeed, it is. My, how I love Earth.' They breathed deeply, even though the street stank of horse dung.

They hailed a hansom cab and helped Ava into it. She was thankful, as she wasn't used to the dress, and crossing sweepers were circling nearby like hunting cats.

The occasional hansom cab, omnibus, or carriage passed by with a clatter of hooves. Ava's eyes were wide, taking in the evening scenery.

'Oh, a lamplighter!' she exclaimed.

The man she had spotted carried a long pole with a lit wick at the end. He was quite quick with it, walking speedily between the lamps to illuminate the dimming streets.

'Indeed. What about it?' Charlemagne asked.

'Well, I've always thought it looked quite fun, but…'

'But what?'

Ava hesitated before saying, 'Madam says it's *unbecoming*.'

'Well, *Madam* isn't here right now.'

Before Ava could stop them, Charlemagne had already signalled the driver to pull over. They produced a coin with a quiet snap of their fingers and handed it through the trapdoor in the ceiling. 'Wait a tick. We'll be returning soon.'

Ava struggled down from the cab after the driver opened the door, waiting for the lamplighter to catch up. 'Pardon me, could I trouble you to allow me to try lighting one of these lamps?'

The lamplighter scrunched his face at Ava, until Charlemagne handed over a sovereign, almost the man's weekly pay. Thus, Ava soon stood below the lamp, holding the surprisingly heavy pole up to the lantern while the lamplighter instructed her.

'Oh look! There's Madam Owens!' Charlemagne said.

Ava's grip loosened and the pole struck the glass wall of the lantern. Shards pelted the cobblestones.

Charlemagne put their hands up. 'Just kidding!'

Ava glared at the grinning demon.

'Oi! Miss, tha's gotta be replaced now!' The man stank of kerosene up close, and seemingly didn't care how finely she was dressed.

'I deeply apologise,' Ava said, panic making her voice and body tremble.

'It doesn't need to be replaced,' Charlemagne said, stepping between the two. Something about their voice felt different, as if there was an unheard echo that made the air shiver.

'It well does! It'll go ou' in wind or rain, and this is London, mind you!'

'Take a look.'

Charlemagne took the pole from Ava, putting it in the lamplighter's hand before leading her back to the cab, as the man stared up in confusion at the unharmed lamp.

'From the country, i' she, sir?' the driver asked half-rhetorically.

Ava blushed at the implied insult. 'That could have gone very badly,' she quietly told Charlemagne.

'It didn't, though.'

'Perhaps not this time, but you can't always magic away consequences.'

'*I* can.' They raised their eyebrows at her, daring her to deny it.

'We'll see.'

Ava was more reserved with her sightseeing after that, although still nothing escaped her curious eye; a woman ignoring an opportunistic crossing sweeper insisting payment; someone almost thrown down by a horse because they didn't look both ways; a crowd of people leaving a theatre after a show. At this, she leaned back in her seat to hide her face.

'Hm? What's this? Is your Madam Owens out there?' Charlemagne asked in a teasing tone. 'What does she look like? I assume you, but older.'

'Why is that?' Ava turned to Charlemagne, her brows furrowed.

'Because you might as well be her, Miss Propriety.'

At this, Ava opened the trap door to speak to the driver. 'To the night market, please.' She turned back to Charlemagne. 'I am *not* Madam Owens.'

Over the sound of clattering and chattering, up-tempo music rose. Ava resisted sticking her head out of the window. As the sound grew, she was finally able to see the source. A man was playing the fiddle for a small crowd of adults and a few children, who were dancing or clapping along. However, he was nearly drowned out by the barkers and hawkers fighting for customers' attention just beyond.

Ava bounced along to the jolly music in her seat, until she sensed something and turned around. A corner of Charlemagne's mouth was pulled up. Were they being sardonic? She lightly slapped their arm. 'Don't you look down on me!'

'I wasn't!' But their grin only widened, revealing razor-sharp teeth once more. 'The music *is* pretty good. Can't get that in Hell.' The last part was muttered under their breath, but Ava still heard.

'I can hardly dance on the street dressed in this fine a gown,' Ava explained, smoothing out the skirts.

'Hardly,' Charlemagne repeated flatly.

Ava narrowed her eyes at them. 'I know your game, and I refuse to play it.'

'Do you, now?'

'I refuse to be goaded.'

'What a shame.' They peered out at the market. 'Ah, I need a hat.' With a snap, a navy green top hat disappeared from a milliner's stall and appeared in Charlemagne's hands.

Ava stared wide-eyed. 'That's stealing! I forbid you to steal!' The demon's amulet at her waist flashed with the command.

Charlemagne pouted. 'Oh, boo you. I thought we were having fun. And besides, I already stole.'

'When?' Ava's tone went up an octave in shock.

'How do you think I paid the lamplighter? And the driver?'

Ava drew in a breath. Her guard had dropped too easily. She shouldn't forget it was not a man she was sitting next to.

'I need to look my best for the ball,' Charlemagne said, putting the top hat on and adjusting it.

'I don't believe social standings matter to a demon.'

'But they do to you.'

Ava blushed. 'Onwards please, driver.'

Finally, the driver announced their arrival at the Verin Rooms, but the exterior wasn't as busy as Ava would've thought. It appeared they had arrived late, around 8pm, which was unsurprising given their detour.

When they entered, a waiter handed Ava a dance card and pencil. The large space was packed, and the music was lively.

Charlemagne took Ava's card and wrote their name on the line for the next dance.

'Shouldn't you ask for my permission first?' Ava said when she took it back.

'Why? Is there someone else you had in mind?'

Ava fought to keep her shoulders and chin up. 'Not particularly. But there will surely be someone.'

'Waiting for your prince, Cinderella? Well, don't let me stop you.' They bowed slightly, one arm behind their waist, the other extending to the ballroom.

Ava watched the dance currently in progress, her shoulders slowly lowering. 'Actually, I think I might not.'

'What? Why not?' Charlemagne seemed genuinely confused, even their nose scrunched up.

'I've only danced at home.'

'You wanted to go to a ball, but not to dance?'

Instead of responding, Ava froze, looking like she had seen a ghost. Ironic, considering her profession. Charlemagne turned to follow her gaze, but couldn't see anyone of note.

'Madam Owens is here,' Ava whispered. 'I must depart. Right away.'

'I have a better idea. Which one is she?'

'The woman wearing burgundy, talking to that gentleman.'

The infamous woman was covered in rings and bracelets, her makeup dark yet alluring on her ageing face. Her brown hair fell in tight ringlets to her chin, a hairstyle more common for younger women.

'Let's have a seat first.'

Charlemagne guided Ava to one of the empty freestanding booths at the side of the room, and took two wine glasses from a nearby waiter, handing one to Ava.

'I haven't…imbibed before.'

'Really? At your age? God, you're sheltered.'

To hide her emotion, Ava took a sip and immediately made a face.

'Burns, doesn't it?' Charlemagne chuckled.

'Indeed.' But she kept sipping anyway. 'What, pray tell, is your better idea?'

'Just watch.'

Thus, the two of them watched as the next dance began, and Madam Owens took to the floor. The men and women lined up for the Roger de Coverley. Ava watched Madam Owens glide around the floor, beaming at her new dance partner as they reeled the line. Looking at her, you wouldn't know she had a little girl waiting for her at home. Ava went to put her glass down on the low table, noticing another empty glass already there. But she hadn't seen Charlemagne drink anything.

When it came time to switch partners again, Madam Owens missed the man's arm, which they quickly resolved. But the slip-up was unmistakable.

'What has happened to her?' Ava asked.

'She appears to be a bit…half-shot. A bit tanked, you might say.' Charlemagne grinned. When Ava cocked her head in confusion, they indicated the now three empty wine glasses on the table.

Ava's mouth gaped, scandalised, but also amused. She took a new full glass that Charlemagne handed to her and sipped.

After a short break, the next dance was a circle waltz, and this time Madam Owens' missteps were far more obvious. She stumbled and staggered, occasionally even tugging at her partner to keep herself upright. Ava giggled, having to cover her mouth to avoid being improper. Eventually, she had to excuse herself, leaving her dance partner to awkwardly exit the dance floor alone.

'Very well, I must be leaving now. That was quite the amusement, Charlemagne, thank you.' Ava downed the last of her wine and went to place the glass down on a waiter's tray. For some reason her arms felt heavy, and the glass clattered far louder than she expected. Unfortunately, while everyone else turned away from the commotion disinterested, Madam Owens locked onto Ava.

The medium strode crookedly across the room towards her, etiquette apparently evading her at this time. 'Dear, whatever are you doing here? You know you can't be out unaccompanied this late! Let's get you home so we can talk about this, hmm?' Her voice was warm and slightly slurred, but her eyes were icicle sharp.

'But I am not unaccompanied.' Ava said quietly.

'Pardon? Dear, you must speak confidently and clearly, it is *most* unbecoming for a woman to mumble. What will people think of how I raised you?'

Charlemagne stepped forward. 'Indeed. What *will* people think?'

Ava turned to them with betrayal in her eyes, but they simply returned her gaze lightly.

Madam Owens' eyes narrowed briefly as she analysed the demon, and then she smiled pleasantly as if she hadn't. 'Forgive me, but I don't believe we've met.' Her voice was honey sweet. 'I am Madam Sylvia Owens, *renowned* spiritual medium. It's a pleasure to make your acquaintance.'

She held out her hand to be kissed, but Charlemagne ignored it. Madam Owens raised an eyebrow, dropped her hand and turned to Ava with her head tilted in concern, but Ava shivered at the masked anger she recognised in the woman's eyes.

'Dear, I have told you many times about the dangers of unknown gentlemen, though I hesitate to call him as such, and their influences. Look at the state of you! Stealing my clothes, drinking alcohol! Goodness, what else have you been up to this evening? Can you even still call yourself a lady? No discernment for male company; next thing you know, you'll be,' she leaned in slightly too close, 'a *dollymop*.' Madam Owens' eyes were glassy, with tiny reflections of Ava in their centres.

Ava's heart dropped. When put that way, she really hadn't been acting like a lady befitting Madam Owens' status this evening. Charlemagne was an actual demon from Hell after all, even if they were under her command. It was a blessing their thefts were untraceable.

Madam Owens sighed and straightened up, shaking her head slightly, and the sweetness leached from her voice. 'Dear, you shall return with me at once, so we may prevent your reputation from falling even further.'

'Who are you to decide this for her?' Charlemagne asked.

'That does not concern you,' Madam Owens said lightly, yet omitting the *sir*.

'Charlemagne shall not leave my side,' Ava stated. She couldn't bear to face her Madam alone right now.

Madam Owens' eyes widened, her hand raised, and she slapped Ava across the cheek. The sound echoed unnaturally, perhaps even *supernaturally*, loudly, and conversation in the ballroom ceased.

'What kind of lady slaps a young girl?' Charlemagne asked, voice projecting like a street performer.

Sylvia Owens stilled as the air filled with hushed discussions, blinking as she realised what she'd done. The woman then convulsed for a few moments, earning gasps from the crowd, before looking around with wide eyes.

'I was overtaken for a moment by a spirit. There is powerful supernatural energy in this room.' Her voice was deep and compelling, that suasive tone the foundation of her career.

'Oh, wow. She's good,' Charlemagne commented quietly. 'Even when drunk.'

'Can she sense you?' Ava was worried. Not that they'd be exposed, but that Madam Owens would be given even more legitimacy and renown.

'Not a damned speck.' Charlemagne raised their voice to address the medium again. 'Isn't it odd for a spirit to suddenly be here, in a public ballroom?'

Madam Owens pulled Ava away from Charlemagne into a side hug, stroking her hair with a limp hand while the other dug its nails into her skin. 'For those uneducated in the matter, it may seem that way. However, the spirit world is as mysterious as it is powerful, as are those that channel it. We must be excused at once so as to not disturb the ball.'

'Oh? Why not put on a show here? Or did you leave your smoke and mirrors at home?'

Madam Owens' nails dug in deeper, and Ava looked to Charlemagne with pleading eyes. Why were they doing this? The demon returned her gaze, simply raising a goading eyebrow.

A gentleman stepped forward from the crowd. 'My good sir, please refrain from interrogating a lady. I happen to be a frequent patron of Sylvia's, and she is truly something to behold.'

Madam Owens sniffed, wiping away a non-existent tear. 'It is alright, Bertram. I am not unaccustomed to such accusations. Suspicion is a burden I must bear when connecting the living with their loved ones on the other side.'

Ava didn't know if it was the alcohol or the indignation that drove her to speak. Perhaps both. She pulled away from the medium and rounded on her.

'You are connecting the living with *me* knocking on the "other side" of the *wall*.'

Madam Owens glared daggers, but Ava didn't let her get a word out. 'You have two light switches for one lightbulb, you make me crawl around in the dark to grab people's legs and knock the table, and your tarot readings are so generic that you could write them prior and hand them out! Dear this, Dear that, do you even remember my name? You won't even let me call you *Mother*!'

Ava was left panting, her throat sore. The room was dead quiet.

Madam Owens leaned in to Ava, 'I raised you to live well in this society.'

Ava's voice was tinged with sadness, 'Then why didn't you let me?' Why was she treated like a manicured rose behind glass?

Bertram panted with anger, having digested what on Earth had just occurred. 'I sold Sir Paul XVII for you! He was a purebred heirloom horse!'

The audience's transfixion broke, and several angry clients emerged from the gossiping crowd. Ava grabbed Charlemagne's hand and ran outside.

'Aren't you supposed to leave a shoe?' they remarked as the pair slowed to a brisk walk.

'This is *not* the time for jokes. Why did you have to make a scene like that?'

'I wasn't the one revealing trade secrets.'

'You know precisely what I mean! Oh, what am I to do?'

'Maybe you could start your own medium business?'

Ava glared at them sidelong.

'Sorry, sorry. I'll stop.' Charlemagne put their hands up in surrender.

After a moment, Ava whispered, 'I've positively destroyed my mother's life. *My* life.' She looked askance at Charlemagne. 'You can't magic that away.'

The pair were silent, sobering up in the hansom cab and the night air, as they made their way back to the Owens house.

The ritual incense was lit in the centre of the drawing room, the scented smoke trailing before Ava's face. 'It appears it is time for me to dismiss you,' she said with a forced professionalism.

'Are you sure?' Charlemagne asked.

'Quite sure.'

'Are you going to be alright?'

'I'll manage,' Ava's voice cracked. She couldn't see how things could possibly get worse.

Charlemagne smiled crookedly. 'If you say so.'

'O spirit Charlemagne, since you have diligently fulfilled my request, I do give you licence to depart. And be ever ready to come at my call.' Her head dropped, her gaze locked uncomfortably on the demon's amulet at her waist. 'I now charge you to withdraw peaceably and quietly, and may the peace of God be ever continued between us. Amen.' The amulet flashed for the last time, and a chill swept across her. Now, Ava would be left to face the future, and Madam Owens, on her own—

'What?'

Ava's head snapped up at Charlemagne's voice.

'I'm still here. You *did* do it correctly, didn't you?'

'Of course I did!' Ava threw the amulet at them in a burst of emotion, and Charlemagne laughed. 'I don't know what I did wrong.'

'Nothing was wrong, silly girl.' The demon's face was childishly smug, 'But just because you dismissed me from your service doesn't mean I have to *leave*. I don't want to.'

'You could *force* me to leave, of course. But you won't,' Charlemagne continued lightly, although Ava was able to hear the edge of concern and fear in their voice, peeking through the bravado.

'You're right,' Ava replied, and she could see the flash of relief on their face. She knew only Hell was waiting for them. And besides, Charlemagne's crimes had only been petty so far. Maybe she could convince them to stop.

With a snap, an especially gaudy jewellery box appeared in their hands. Charlemagne smiled wickedly. 'Let's take your inheritance early, shall we?'

Ava frowned, but didn't object. 'And do what?'

'Anything we want.' Charlemagne flashed their sharp teeth.

The Eulogy of Alice Adams

Maddy Nyp

Devon – 1952

On the day her Godmother died, Chardonay forgot to buy a loaf of bread.

Chardonay knew it was a foolish oversight. There, on her shopping list, between the milk and the apples, was *bread* underlined and circled. Her Godmother, Alice, loved bread, but that hadn't prevented their last loaf from becoming mouldy. Did that mean she shouldn't buy bread? Would it just be a waste? Chardonay couldn't stomach gluten, so had almost left it off, but Alice had moaned something like *toast* from the bed she would soon die in, and she didn't have the heart to say no. So, she'd underlined and circled it, paranoid shopper was she, and assumed her penmanship wouldn't let her down.

Alice died two minutes before midday, and Chardonay returned to her side five minutes past: breadless, beaten, bewildered. She had seen two corpses in her life, but still, it surprised her how quickly a body stopped being a person and became just another *thing*. Bedside lamp, table, dead body. Alice wasn't here, she wasn't in this house, she wasn't in this room. Alice had been a vessel of exuberant light, and now she had gone somewhere else; Chardonay could feel it.

Chardonay paid the medical bill. Chardonay left the room. Chardonay threw up in the toilet, then dialled Alice's sister. No one picked up and she sat on the floor: alone, alone, alone.

Alice's death did not deter life's arrow. The doctors took her body, and the Angels her soul—both sprinting away from Chardonay at an alarming rate. Chardonay was left in Bovey Tracey; a place where self-reflection was all too imminent.

Chardonay wondered if she had been born an embarrassment, or if it had been a disease she had caught, akin to the sickness that had taken Alice in the end. In the days that followed her Godmother's death, Chardonay decided it had been the former, for she could not remember a moment of life where she had been anything but. Alice had worked hard to turn her into someone respectable; Chardonay could not fault her upbringing for how she developed.

After Alice died, Chardonay stayed in Bovey Tracey. Once, Chardonay had dreams of becoming a painter and moving to London as all the great artists must. But her Godmother's illness had eaten up the years Chardonay could have used studying and gobbled down what little savings she had tucked away. Not that Chardonay minded; Alice had taken her after the war, which had made orphans of so many, and selflessly raised her as a daughter. Besides, being an artist was a fool's dream—another symptom of the disease Chardonay had been born with.

Chardonay had been left explicit instructions on how to deal with a post-Alice world. She had staggered through organising cousins for the funeral, but when the time came, Chardonay had not attended. Alice had not wanted her to. Chardonay supposed she didn't deserve to go; she had missed her final moments with Alice, after all.

Each night the grief whispered: *where were you?*

Buying bread, Chardonay would reply. But that was a terrible answer, and the grief cackled.

There was one thing Chardonay knew to hold on to. One request that even she could not get wrong:

'Bring the photo album to my grave,' Alice had once told her over a game of chess. Chardonay had always loved the game, but loved seeing her Godmother's eyes light with their old spark even more. 'Don't go to my funeral. Wait until afterwards, then break into the graveyard for me, and leave the album.'

Chardonay moved her knight to E4. It was a losing move, but Alice never appreciated it when she won. 'I will, Godmother.'

'Do not forget, and don't be lazy about it either,' Alice had huffed and beamed at the board. 'Foolish move. Checkmate.'

On the eighth of May, Chardonay got in her Godmother's car, Morris, and drove out of Bovey

Tracey. Now, sitting at the bottom of the road that led through moorland and into the village of Widecombe, Chardonay let the old car pause. What right did life have to parade itself, only two months after her Godmother had died? Though, whatever the weather, this part of the Moors had always spooked her. The grass was snakelike and long, the hills steep and bumpy, and the bracken like a rude lady's face glaring from where it scattered. The same pretty world, though perhaps a little darker, a little less innocent.

Chardonay did not want to go to the grave. She did not want to stand on the burial ground; she did not want to look down and imagine her Godmother in a coffin, stuffed and prim in the dress she'd asked to be buried in. It made a sickness fog the edges of her vision and threaten to choke the tongue out of her throat. But this was what Alice would have wanted. She ran her fingers idly across the steering wheel, in what may have been a soothing motion, if she hadn't been distracted by the lump on the hill.

The lump was plum-faced and round, stumbling and tripping up the Moors. As it walked, Chardonay realised the lump wasn't a strange horse or lost dog, but a child. A child with black hair and pretty pigtails, a child who was about to enter the heart of Widecombe.

Chardonay knew that a child lost to the Moors was a child lost forever. That was why she didn't hesitate, didn't even blink, and sprinted out the car door, her hair flying in the tangled breeze.

At the top of the first hill, Chardonay bent double and took a series of heaving breaths (Alice had always told her to stay in shape!). There was no child in sight. The grass, so tall and thick, shielded the Moor's underworld too well. She was about to assume herself mad, most mourners were, but then she heard the squeal.

Like a bloodhound to the scent, Chardonay followed the sound. There—just ahead, something on the ground. Chardonay beat towards it, arms pumping and feet slapping. She knew she was fast; Alice had always said she was proficient at running away.

As flies scavenge around a carcass, black ravens circled a girl, collapsed on the ground with her hands over her head. One bird darted down and nipped the girl's leg, and she let out a sob.

Thinking fast, Chardonay hopped onto one leg and violently pulled off her shoe. With all the aim of a sleep-deprived mourner, she chucked the offending object at the nearest bird. The thing screamed as if it had been shot and pelted back towards the sky—stupid creatures. Anyone born near the Moors would tell you the birds were cowards at heart. The second someone protested their attack, the group turned and fled, the sun bouncing off their glossy black pelts.

Chardonay tripped and stumbled over to the girl, who was rubbing dirt off her face and peering up at the world with round eyes. 'Bloody hell, are you okay?'

The girl blinked at her. She wore strange clothing, a simple white frock, and had a familiarity Chardonay couldn't quite place. 'Don't say bloody. Mamma gives us the paddle when we say bloody.'

Chardonay felt shame prickle down her spine. Alice often told her the same thing: that her uncouth language would never attract a man, nor help her find a position in good society. Her Godmother would laugh, perhaps, to see a child no older than ten already knew the things Chardonay was supposed to.

The girl had dropped a large, lumpy rucksack. Chardonay bent and picked it up, spying a loaf of bread and a bottle of juice tucked neatly inside. 'Are you hurt?'

'Nope!' The girl grinned toothlessly. 'Glad you came along, though. You gotta good arm! Those birds were scary. I didn't even do anything to them!'

'They were probably nesting,' Chardonay offered evenly. 'Where's your mum and dad?'

'Still asleep back home.'

'And where's home?'

'Widecombe,' The girl stuck out her chin. 'I'm running away!'

'Sorry, did you come all this way yourself?'

The girl's eyes lit up, 'Yep!'

Odd. 'What's your name?'

The girl crossed her arms. 'I'm not supposed to give my name to strangers.'

That was... fair, Chardonay supposed. She forced a smile, 'I'm Chardonay.'

'That's a funny name.'

It was. Chardonay had been named after a birthmark on her back, spotted and snow-white, as if God had broken a bottle over her spine. It was one of those funny oddities Alice enjoyed collecting, a strange story to tell over dinner parties. Chardonay sighed, 'C'mon, I'm taking you back to your parents. I'm heading to Widecombe myself; it isn't out of my way.'

'No!'

'Yes,' Chardonay replied. This is why she never wanted children. During the only real fight they'd ever had, when Chardonay was eight and foolish, Alice had snapped that no one really liked kids, that they were vain and imprudent. Alice had been right, of course. 'I'm taking you home, or you don't get the rucksack back.'

'But that's mine! You're a thief!'

'Tough,' Chardonay replied. 'I do need a new rucksack. I suppose I should just take this one...'

'Okay.' The kid pouted. 'Adults are mean, you know that, right?'

'I do. Come on, I'll give you a lift.'

Chardonay led the silent girl back to Morris and gestured for her to sit in the front; the second package she would now be delivering to Widecombe. Chardonay felt like yelling at her reflection in the rear-view mirror. Surely, this endeavour would only delay bringing Alice's album to her grave? God, she couldn't bother to turn up for Alice's final moments, and now she was getting *this* wrong!

Chardonay sighed, 'Where do you live?'

'Next to the church. These are pretty!' the girl said. To Chardonay's shock, the girl had laid Alice's photo album on her lap. 'Are they yours?'

'Careful with that!' Chardonay scooped up the book and held it close. The girl blinked as if Chardonay had committed the most unreasonable act in the world. 'It's very fragile!'

'It doesn't look fragile.'

Truth be told, Chardonay had always disliked the book. It housed hundreds of photos from Alice's life: the day she bought Morris, dinner parties at Bovey Tracey, pictures from her third wedding. She had asked Alice to photograph her once, and her Godmother had firmly stated she would have a picture when the time was right, but not a second before. Chardonay supposed the time had never been right, for there was nothing of her inside.

'It just is,' Chardonay replied lamely, turning over the engine and pulling onto the road. 'Why were you running away?'

The girl drew her finger against the glass, tracing the bracken and spindly trees that started to mark the hills. 'I had a fight with Ma.'

'Must have been some fight.'

'She's just...she's so mean! She's meaner than you. She keeps treating me like I'm old. I'm not old,' the girl puffed out her cheeks and crossed her arms. 'She gets so angry when I get things wrong.'

'She treats you like an adult?'

'Mamas don't make sense...WOAH WHAT'S THAT!'

Chardonay slammed the breaks. The car lurched forward, gravel spewing and the content of the backseat briefly gaining air. The girl was tugging the handle of the door excitedly as Chardonay drew breath, then looked incredulously at the child. 'What do you think you're doing! Don't yell when an adult is driving!'

The girl wasn't listening. Instead, her attention belonged out the window. Roadside, a group of four fat ponies munched on the grass and bracken, their grey pelts blending in with the rocky ground and gravel road. Chardonay could see a little of Widecombe poking out behind them, tantalisingly close.

'ARE THOSE HORSES?'

'Don't yell,' Chardonay replied flatly.

The girl turned to her, beaming, 'Can we go see them?'

'No, definitely not.'

The girl looked close to screaming again. 'You're no fun!'

'We'll scare them off,' Chardonay said quickly. 'They're Dartmoor ponies, see. They get scared off by people. No one touches them, we just get to look. It would make them very sad if we interrupted them.'

'Oh,' the girl blinked. 'That's okay, then. I don't want the ponies to be sad. I can draw a horse, did you know that? I wanna be an artist when I grow up. Here, look at this!'

The girl fished in her rucksack, pushing aside the crumbly bread and what may have been a toy elephant before tugging out a notebook and a single pink crayon. Chardonay, dimly aware that the afternoon was starting to drag, made a slight sound of protest, but it fell on deaf ears.

Alice had told her that being an artist was difficult. Her argument had been convincing: Chardonay would have no money, and would be too far away from her Godmother to assist her with cleaning, and would never have the discipline to properly study.

'See!' The girl held up a crude crayon drawing of a pony. It was bright red, and the lines were practically scribbles. 'See! I'm pretty good, aren't I?'

She wasn't, but her grin was infectious, and Chardonay could feel it play on the corner of her mouth. 'Not bad. But being an artist is hard, right? Artists don't make much money.'

'Yeah, they do!' The girl huffed, sinking back into Morris's leather seats. 'I'm gonna be the best artist in the world, you just watch!'

Chardonay's rebuttal to Alice had been similar. Chardonay couldn't quite remember what Alice had said next. What would have she wanted to hear at that age?

'Alright. You be an artist, then.'

Widecombe was a passerby village to all but those who knew her. As one of those lucky few, Chardonay knew to abandon Morris behind the pub. To Chardonay's surprise, the girl practically dove out the car, snatching her bag along the way, and eagerly pulled Chardonay by hand towards the church. Figuring she had to be the vicar's daughter, and intending to reach the grave regardless, Chardonay followed.

The last time Chardonay had visited the church was just before she had moved to Bovey

Tracey. The chapel was still tall and proud, gazing warmly through her great clock, and offering a smile with twinkling stained glass. Next to her, a graveyard rested. Perhaps it was once orderly, but after the war it had become haphazard. Tomb stones broke out of the earth wherever they could stuff a body, weeds tangled over what was once a pathway, and cat grass covered the weak fence separating Moors from chapel lands.

The girl moved between graves with the confidence of a seasoned ballerina. Eventually she stopped at a rather large one, the inscription new and blazing. Chardonay felt a chill pass the entire way through her as she reached it.

1905-1952

ALICE ADAMS

Belived by all.

Impossibly, Chardonay's throat tightened. She'd imagined this grave a million times, but seeing it was a different beast. Thousands of thoughts spilled through her head, but all Chardonay could say was, 'They misspelt *Beloved*. She'd kill me if she knew.'

'Really?' The girl tilted her head to the side, 'That's not very nice. Hey, what's that funny thing behind the grave?'

Chardonay blinked, noticing that there was indeed a strange bit of paper seemingly taped to the back of the stone, blessed with a perfect view of the moorland. With a trembling hand, Chardonay reached and tugged it towards her.

The painting was not particularly good. The line art shook and sprawled, the paper was too rich for the ink to properly settle, and the colouring was a little saturated, an odd homage a Van Gogh and his abstract impressionism. But the artist's hands had trembled in the end, and her eyesight had failed alongside her liver, so Chardonay supposed she shouldn't judge. Signed in the corner, a shaky AA.

Chardonay's Godmother had drawn *her*.

Knowing she couldn't support herself much longer, Chardonay sunk to the ground; the ground beneath which carried her Godmother, the ground that could at least do the job of supporting her when nothing else could.

To be so close but so far away. Suddenly, Chardonay felt eight again; a lost child at the markets, bumbling around and desperate for attention.

'But she hated drawings!' Chardonay clutched at the page like a toddler might a favoured toy. 'Who left this here—how did anyone get this? It wasn't with her things. You live around here, don't you? Did you see the funeral? Did someone, what, tape it here?'

'Nope!'

'But you said you lived by the church.'

And Alice shrugged, 'Yeah, but I'm not really here, am I? Remember? I died.'

Oh.

Chardonay looked at the girl, and the girl looked at Chardonay. In that moment, as the girl and mourner considered each other, Chardonay finally understood.

Oh.

The tightening of her throat turned to a rich burn, but still the tears that threatened her eyelids did not let.

Oh.

A million swirling thoughts competed for victory in the storming moorland that was Chardonay's head, but she settled on the one she could vocalise: 'How are you here? Or is this all in my head?'

Alice tilted her head. 'Dunno, really. What do you think?'

Chardonay wasn't quite sure what to think. In fact, the very concept of thought seemed insignificant in the face of whatever this thing was—spirit, spectre, something similarly sinister. Perhaps she was mad, perhaps that was it. The girl opened her rucksack, plucking a slice of the loaf with bits of cheese in the crust, and took a bite. Perhaps it wasn't important. It felt real enough to Chardonay, and maybe that was all one could say on the matter.

Chardonay hesitated, glancing at the grave, 'I'm sorry that, y'know—'

'Don't say "y'know," it makes you sound American.'

Despite the severity of the situation, Chardonay almost rolled her eyes. So, it was Alice, then. 'I'm sorry you died.'

'Everything dies,' Alice took another bite, 'I lived a happy life, didn't I? I got to be a mum.'

'I feel like I let you down a lot,' Chardonay ran a hand through her hair, tugging at the wiry ends. 'Especially now.'

'I don't think I could be disappointed in someone who loved me so much.'

Chardonay swallowed thickly, 'I wasn't there when you died.'

'It's okay.'

'No, it isn't!' Chardonay furiously scrubbed the tears clinging to her cheeks, 'You died alone. You weren't supposed to die alone!'

'Maybe,' Alice said carefully, 'I wanted to die alone. Maybe I didn't want you to see. Have you considered that?'

'Did you love me enough for that?'

'Evidently.' Alice looked offended. 'I know I could be selfish. I know that. But maybe, at the end, I wanted to do something for you instead.'

Part of Chardonay wondered if Alice only viewed her as a job to be fulfilled. Some days, she had certainly acted like Chardonay was another assignment, up there with knitting for charity and putting Morris in for a service. What was the love of a mother, really? Was it the cage that holds the bird, safe and comfortable, yet always stagnant?

Chardonay narrowed her eyes. 'You only took me in because you wanted someone else to look after you, and I couldn't even do that right! I was supposed to be perfect. And I wasn't. And I'm not.'

Alice placed a hand on her shoulder soothingly. 'You don't have to be perfect—'

'Don't I? Because you never approved of me right up until you died.'

Alice didn't answer. Chardonay hadn't expected her to. There was no closure to be found here.

And that was the truth of it. Mother and child, girl and daughter, considered each other. Would Chardonay have children? Would she reach Alice's age, and look in the mirror, and suddenly see her adoptive mother: the good, the bad, nothing new, the same face and weariness. Was motherhood a circle, then; the same actors on a stage, recast and recast?

Finally, Alice pursed her lips, 'Why do you need my approval?'

'Because you're you!' Chardonay blinked furiously, the tears brimming on her eyelashes like dew in a spider's web. 'Because you were perfect, so I had to be. I had to be, and I can't do it!'

'I'm not perfect. I'm eight.'

Chardonay looked at the girl, truly looked at her. The blemishes on her skin, the frayed ends of hair, the bits of dirt on the edges of her frock. It startled Chardonay to think of Alice like this, so young and so reckless, two things she'd never been in Chardonay's life. It was a strange realisation to suddenly see a parent as human.

'I wanted you to be ready for when I was dead,' Alice said bluntly. 'I'm sorry. I got it wrong.'

'Yeah,' Chardonay scrubbed under her eyes. 'Yeah, you did.'

'I wasn't perfect. Not now and not then. But I loved you a lot. Look how I drew you!'

Chardonay stared at the grave. She thought of all the little ways she had let Alice down over her life, but then again, she had been a child herself. Had she been sick, or had she just been sixteen, and not fully ready to take on the world? Chardonay didn't know. She could not remember a time when she had been treated as someone Alice's age now.

'Do you miss me?'

'You were the only mother I ever had. Of course I miss you.'

Alice scooted over and laid her head on her adoptive daughter's shoulder. 'I wanna be a painter when I grow up.'

Alice had given her a life, but it was not a life Chardonay had asked for. They had let each other down, mother and daughter: Alice had taken painting, Chardonay had taken a comforting hand at the end. There was suddenly a million things Chardonay wanted to say to the woman, all of them rushing through her at once. That opportunity was gone, now. If Alice was alive, would Chardonay's life be better? She wasn't sure, only that the regret was bitter, and formed a congealed lump at the back of her throat.

But then again, Chardonay forgot, some days, that her Godmother had been a child, too. That perhaps her Godmother was simply Alice: a complicated figure, but maybe most importantly, a human one. Her approval was not the making of Chardonay; her approval could not be the tightrope Chardonay's life balanced on.

Chardonay sat and stared at the headstone. Pulling the album out of her pocket, she threw it at the grave. It bounced off the tombstone and flopped on the ground. But she did keep the painting, folded and cuddled in her pocket. It could live in her own sketchbook perhaps; as much closure on Alice expected she would ever find.

To herself, Chardonay replied: 'You know what? I do, too.'

You're So Cool

Indigo James

Adelaide, Australia – 1972

I have a theory about hair. The bigger it is, the bigger your ego. Charlie's honeycomb spiralled curls are as big as her presence. I have always envied her. The way she can wake up in the morning, in a beaten-up old t-shirt and look...good? Maybe my jealousy is why I made excuses for her behaviour, the manipulation, the mind games. Both are easy to overlook as she emits her infectious charm that makes you feel *special*. It's like a glow. A spotlight hot on your face. Little did I know that the spotlight only appears when you are useful to her.

Charlie is a concoction of contradictions. She proclaims to be a feminist visionary like Gloria Steinem, but is always in competition with the women around her. She acts like a struggling artist, yet comes from a family that would cover her every financial request. She claims to be my best friend, but sometimes I wonder if our definitions of the term differ. Maybe, without the continual support and attention I deliver, it would be a different story all together.

I think her idea of heaven would be standing on a stage surrounded by fans worshipping her. And for me? Well, I'd rather die.

To some, it probably doesn't make much sense why Charlie and I are best friends. I guess you could say growing up two streets apart is the reason. Or my desperate need to feel like someone *really* gets me.

Charlie rang earlier to invite me to come round for tea. It takes a solid four minutes to walk there. I used to always feel excited to see her, but now I've got this sinking sensation of *dread*.

I can hear her favourite Stones record playing, *Let It Bleed*. I knock twice, gently. No response. I huff and bang my knuckles three times on the door. It never is simple reaching Charlie.

The door swings open, pot smoke flooding out.

'Ally, babe!' she exclaims.

Judging by the scene, Charlie's parents are out of town. Her family is way cooler than mine—they don't push her in a strict direction. If she decided to join a commune, they wouldn't bat an eyelid. My parents are more conservative and would totally *freak out* if I ever even mentioned something so radical. She gestures for me to join her on the rug, amongst her sprawled out records.

'Where are Lisa and Arthur?' I ask.

'Up the shack for their anniversary.' She removes the joint from her lips, offering me a toke. I hesitate and, as if reading my mind, she announces, 'Forget study tonight, just stay over, chill out and take a hit, babe.' I give in and shrug off my brewing anxiety. She eases herself back onto the rug and winks, 'Atta girl.'

I awaken to the smell of cinnamon toast and Jefferson Airplane on the radio. Charlie is perched on the kitchen counter and hands me a plate, dangling her legs eagerly.

'So, I reckon we should go down to Allen's Record Store this morning and check out their new releases,' she says.

I begin mentally listing all the things I need to finish for class tomorrow, but her gaze pleads with me to oblige. 'Alright, just an hour or two.'

Charlie hops off the bench. 'Groovy. I want to see if they've got the latest Doors album yet.'

She tosses me a purple cheesecloth dress to throw on. We hop in her mustard VW Beetle, which always smells like old leather and tobacco.

'So, this essay I've been working on, we have to analyse a play. It's called *Waiting for Godot*. It's really interesting. It symbolises enduring suffering through companionship and the passing of time. It's really been making me think about life, you know.'

She lights a cigarette, inhales and blows the smoke directly in my face.

'Did you hear anything I just said?'

'Hold this, I need to re-apply my lippy.' Charlie passes the cigarette to me and removes the metal cap of her plum lipstick. POP. She stares into the mirror and begins applying, dragging the edges of her sharp nails along the outer corners of her mouth to fix any imperfections.

'Charlie?'

'Ugh. It's too early for existentialism, Ally. Now pass me back that cigarette.'

God, I am sick to death of feeling like her servant.

When we pull up to Allen's, I am instantly greeted by the sweet smell of frankincense and a big box of second-hand records for sale out the front. Then, all of a sudden, I see Charlie's ex-boyfriend, Mick, standing at the register. My stomach sinks. Shit. Since when did he start working here?

For context, Mick had a habit of sleeping with girls behind Charlie's back and broke her ~~heart~~ ego.

Charlie turns to me, 'Shit, do I look okay?'

I roll my eyes. 'Who cares what he thinks?'

Charlie is strong in every sense of the word, but rejection is something her brain cannot comprehend. She would get back with him in a heartbeat, just to dump him, in order to have the upper hand. Yes, he's a talented musician, but a lousy boyfriend.

Of course, she ignores my advice yet again, and walks straight up to him.

'Since when did you get back in town?'

He smirks. 'Missed me, darlin'?'

I walk as far away from them as possible. Unfortunately, I hear everything. Charlie doesn't understand the concept of an inside voice.

She eventually returns with that wild look in her eyes and a devilish grin painted on her face. 'Alright! All done. Let's go.'

'Hang on, I haven't even got my record yet,' I snap.

'Hurry up then, we don't have all day, babes.'

'Charlie, I'll be like two seconds.'

Charlie rolls her eyes and I feel my anxiety peak once again.

She was the one who suggested we come here. I pick up Joni Mitchell's latest record, *Blue,* from the pile and position it under my arm. Mick's eyes gaze down at my chest as I walk to the register.

'Well, if it isn't Little Miss Ally. How's that big girl degree of yours coming along?'

'Fine. Just this one, thanks.'

He takes the record and inspects it, before asking, 'Any fellas on the scene for you? My mate Bill loves a girl with big knockers.'

'How lovely.'

'A lady of few words, huh, Ally?'

'I save up my words for those worthy.'

Mick glances at Charlie and they both laugh.

Mockingly.

As we're driving back, Charlie wastes no time filling me in on the explicit detail of the exchange between her and Mick. I nod, with some 'uh huh's' thrown in there, to seem somewhat interested.

'So, he's invited me to see him play at this coffee lounge tonight. You're coming with me and I'm not taking no for an answer.'

I can't hold in the groan, it comes out involuntarily.

She furthers her argument. 'It's not like you've got any other plans, is it, Grandma? Besides, you need to get out there and meet someone eventually.'

'I thought it was 1972 and we were all about...liberation for women? Since when do I *need* a man?' I say.

'Oh, calm down babes, that's not the point.'

I don't have the energy to respond to her this time.

'That's what I thought. Now, to more important matters. I need your expert opinion on what I should wear. You always know best don't you, Ally babes. It's why I love you.' Charlie winks.

There she goes again, attempting to pull me back in.

Making me feel special. It works too easily on me.

'I want to look hot as fuck.' She begins listing all her options and begs that I rate each outfit from one to ten. The fact she doesn't even notice that I'm frustrated with her is what sends me over the edge.

How can someone be *this* self-absorbed?

How can I call this person my *best* friend?

As we pull up to her place and get out of the car, I slam the door.

'He was such an asshole to you, Charlie. Why put yourself through that *again*?'

Of all the reactions she could have, she starts smiling. 'People make mistakes and...things were getting a little boring around here.'

I roll my eyes. I assume Charlie finally notices she's losing my sympathy and instinctively shifts character. A character that I've come to know quite well.

The baby voice. The sunken shoulders. The pleading.

All designed to guilt me.

'Please, you know I can't go without you.' Quivering her lip.

Now I'm stuck. Charlie knows guilt is one of my biggest driving forces when it comes to decision making. 'Fine, but I can't stay long.'

I hate myself for giving in to her again.

The coffee lounge is cool, I'll give her that. It's dripping with Parisian atmosphere. There are little nooks with velvet pillows and hanging tapestries, and a haze of rich incense and marijuana filling the room, amongst the low hum of conversations. Everyone down here is smoking something and drinking chinotto or red wine.

Charlie starts anxiously applying patchouli oil to her wrists and neck, 'I'm going to say hi to Mick. Wanna come with?' She translates my death stare as a 'no' and walks off.

I look over my shoulder to scan the room, comparing myself to everyone around me. There are so many cool people down here. Trendy couples kissing and giggling. Free spirited girls with hair below their waist, rocking high waisted denim flares and platform boots, with a cigarette in one hand and glass in the other. I don't have the cool factor. That *edge*.

I notice a girl from my English Lit class. She's sitting alone in one of the little nooks, writing in a tattered brown notebook. I'm pretty sure her name starts with a C. She looks up and sees me, smiles and then waves. I turn around to check the wave was directed at me but there's no one behind me. I wave back.

I feel my anxiety start to dissipate.

Charlie quickly struts back over to me and asks, 'Who was *that*?'

'Oh...that's just a girl from my English lit class. She seems really nice.'

I notice Charlie's eyes twitch, ever so slightly as she looks her up and down.

Is she...*jealous?*

'Hoooow cute! Miss Ally babes has a little friend,' she says.

She flicks her hair, as if attempting to shake off an emotion.

It's in these moments—these tiny, fleeting moments—where I remind myself that she *does* care.

It never lasts, though.

To no surprise, Mick ends up dedicating his final song to her, 'This one's for a special foxy lady in the crowd.'

I cringe but I can feel her heart fluttering next to me.

Like a moth to a flame, Charlie eagerly rushes over to him at the end of his performance, smooching his cheek. She looks around and devours the attention she receives being with *him*.

I take the last few sips of my chinotto as she waltzes back over to me.

'Alright! We're heading to one of Mick's mate's places.'

'You know I can't, I've got study.'

Her lips form a pout, 'La-la-la Miss Lame-O.'

'I'd rather that then being a groupie for a bunch of misogynists.'

Except, I say it to her back. She's already walking away, arm in arm with Mick, waltzing out of the lounge.

I knew I shouldn't have come here tonight.

The next morning, the phone rings. I rush to the lounge room, but Mum already has the phone in her hand, 'Yes, she's here.'

She hands me the phone with a disapproving glance, 'It's Charlie'.

Before I can even get a word in, Charlie's on a tangent about her night. She mentions all the cool, progressive people she met, the writers and artists and musicians. She continues, relaying to me, how they all told her just how brilliant she is.

'I'm just saying, you missed out big time. Such a pity.'

My patience grows thin and I zone out. I wonder if she will maybe ask how I'm going? Or God forbid, just ask me *anything?*

'Look, I've gotta go, Charlie. Mum needs the phone and I've got—'

Charlie releases a dramatic sigh, cutting me off, 'I know you're getting all smart and whatnot but don't forget about your friends.'

That's rich, I think to myself. 'Well don't forget why Mick is a fucking jerk,' I say. I hang up and suddenly realise Mum is looking at me in shock, as if I've just committed every sin in the Bible. I rush back into my room, closing the door quietly, and sink to the floor.

The next morning, I check the letterbox and see a note:

Sick of fighting with you, Ally babes.
Let me make it up to you.
Mum's making lamb casserole tonight, the one you love!

Come round
Love, C xoxo

After spending the day working on my essay, I catch a bus home. I can't help but find parallels between the texts I'm critiquing and my life. Perhaps I'm Vladimir and Charlie is Estragon. Are we bound to each other in a relationship of dependency?

Is Charlie right, am I missing out on life?

The bus comes to a halt, along with my scattered thoughts. When I get to Charlie's, I notice her car isn't parked in the street. Weird.

Arthur greets me with a grin on his face, 'Well hello there, Ally! What brings us the pleasure?'

'Is Charlie home? She invited me round for tea.'

His smile shifts to concern. 'We assumed she was with you?'

I lie to calm his nerves. 'I was with her earlier but had study to finish, I'm sure she'll be home soon.'

He invites me in and I join Lisa in the kitchen.

Thirty minutes pass and she still isn't home. Arthur attempts to smile through his disappointment, 'Well, we can't let the food get cold now, can we? We can keep hers warm in the oven.'

After an hour, we've finished dinner and I've run out of questions about their anniversary. Despite being pissed off, I'm now worried. I feel responsible for her safety, her whereabouts and the repercussions of her actions. I sound like I'm her mum. Ugh.

I hate that my sense of obligation overrides my own feelings.

Eventually, through the window, I see Charlie's car pull into the driveway. She staggers to the door, drunk or stoned, I presume. Or both.

'Smells delish, Mama!'

'Where the hell have you been?' I spit.

Stumbling into me, she presses her finger on my lips. 'Shhhhh. Chill, babe. I was with Mick and his bandmates talking music y'know. It was a blast!'

I can't believe it. Yet again, she is incapable of realising how selfish she is. 'Well, some warning would've been nice,' I bite back.

She giggles, 'Ally, for Christ's sake, you need to get laid, girl!'

Her parents finally cut in, 'Charlie!'

Charlie opens her purse, pulling out a joint, 'Anyone got a light?'

Fuming, I storm outside and slam the door behind me. I can feel a thick volcanic rage building inside me. Images begin to flood my mind of all the things she has done over the years; the mocking, belittling and emotional manipulation.

Charlie follows me. Her face is smirking, as if all of this is amusing to her, 'On the rags, babes?'

I turn around and say nothing at first. I let her experience the uncertainty, the lack of control she must feel.

'I don't owe you shit, Ally! I have no obligation to you.'

I snap. 'No, Charlie, you *don't*.'

I keep walking and she runs to stop me.

'I think you're projecting, Ally babes. You're still not over your Daddy dying, are you? I think you're putting all of that onto me...and I didn't ask for that.'

I turn around slowly to face her.

'What the *fuck* is wrong with you?'

'I'm just saying. This is all a bit much for me, I just wanted to have a fun night and now I'm being yelled at. Let's just start the night over, you can stay over—'

'Why did you even invite me over? You wanted to make it up to me, remember? You still expect me to do whatever you want, like I'm this sweet, docile, puppy for you to play with. Just be honest for once in your life and admit that you're a shit friend. That you don't give a fuck about me or anyone.'

She doesn't say anything back to that.

'I looked up to you, Charlie. I thought you were the coolest person I had ever met. You made me feel as if I had something to offer the world. Now, I look at you and I see someone who is deeply insecure. You *need* other people to feel better about yourself, and I'm sick of being that person.'

Her eyes swell up with tears, but this time I don't let the guilt win.

'It's been a really tough year for me Ally, you know this. You know I had the breakup with Mick and Dad has been acting weird lately...I think Mum and Dad might even split up.'

I've successfully broken the pattern because no part of me feels bad, or guilty, or responsible. It merely sounds like background noise as I walk home. I don't turn around once.

I wake up to my brain on a feedback loop, skipping over each word that was exchanged.

Will I regret this?

Who am I, *without her?*

Out of the corner of my eye, I notice my new record and pick it up. I remove it from the plastic slip and place it on my player, carefully dropping the needle on the record. I light a candle and allow the thoughts to drift away. I feel Joni's melodies embracing me, easing my worries one by one.

When I arrive on campus, I head straight to the library to study. I take a seat at the back of the room and arrange my things on the table: notepad, papers and theory books. I begin writing, and notice the same girl from my English Lit class walking into the library. She sits at the table across from me and smiles.

'It's Ally, right? I'm Clara. We're in the same class,' she says.

'Hey! I remember, I saw you at the gig last Friday,' I respond.

'I wasn't sure you'd remember! Did you have fun?' she asks.

'Ahh...not quite.'

'Me either, it was one big group of pretentious assholes.'

'Exactly!'

'Are you working on the Lit paper, too?' she asks.

'Sure am. I love the text but it's hard to articulate such big concepts in the minimal word count.'

'I'm finding that, too. Mind if I sit with you? We could trade notes...if you want?'

I smile and gesture for her to sit next to me, 'Of course!'

'Professor Dutton is kinda cute, don't you think?' she asks.

'Any man with an appreciation for feminist literature has my heart.'

'Professor Cleary on the other hand...'

'Now that man needs to trim his eyebrows.'

We burst into laughter and the librarian aggressively hushes us. It only makes us laugh more.

We spend the next two hours talking about our favourite theorists, authors and concepts. I realise that in these two hours, Clara has asked me more things about myself than Charlie ever has. I feel lighter around Clara, freer. It feels as if she *gets* me.

After she finishes scanning through the pages of her essay, she turns to me.

'Favourite author?' she asks.

'Virginia Woolf. Yours?'

'Germaine Greer,' she responds.

'Great answer,' I say.

'What's your star sign?' she asks.

'I'm a Libra. What's yours?'

'I love Libras! I'm an Aquarius. Who's your favourite singer?' she asks.

'Hmm... I'd have to say Joni Mitchell. Her lyrics are so...raw.'

'I figured. You're so cool.'

'I don't think anyone has ever called me cool before,' I respond.

She chuckles, 'As if.'

Out of the spirit of newfound confidence I make a suggestion, 'Well, should we get a drink or something to celebrate finishing these damn essays?'

'Fantastic idea. The Uni Bar has a new jukebox that plays cool tunes,' she says.

'Perfect. Let's dance.' I say, grinning.

Under the Same Water
Ez Knill

Brooklyn, New York City – December, 1996

It's yellow. A really, really fucking ugly shade of yellow. The *only* 24-hour laundromat close to Andy's apartment and it's a migraine-inducing eyesore of a building. It's obvious that the owner was trying to disguise the water stains and mould growing through the plaster. It hasn't worked. Inside, the scuffed machines, rusted and old as they are, sit tiled tight against the fresh paint.

'Well,' she says to Chuckle, even though he's curled around her shoulders and asleep, 'It's certainly…cheerful.'

He doesn't respond, of course, but for once she hadn't expected him to. It's rare that a word between them is spoken aloud, what with the nature of a witch's bond with her familiar. Telepathy is a tricky spell to master, normally, but the connection between witch and her true familiar, her soul-creature, supersedes that difficulty.

Andy sighs, plucks the cigarette from behind her ear and balances it between her lips. Rooting around her bag, she pulls out the half-empty BIC she'd stolen from the corner store on Myrtle Avenue and flicks it, catching the tip of her cigarette in the flame.

The washing basket settles further into the crease of her waist as she trudges to the nearest available washer, a plume of smoke drifting lazily from the cherry-red end. She glances out the window as she rummages around her bag to find the coins loose at the bottom, counts out seventy-five cents and stacks them into a little pile on the bench next to her basket.

It's already dark outside, and the glare of fluorescent strip lighting is bathing the laundromat in unforgiving white, bouncing off the garish yellow. The hours of sunlight had been growing steadily shorter as the days curled sweetly into December, and this day was no exception. The sun had decided to die along the horizon line as Andy reached the laundromat, at only just past six. Andy breaths out around the cigarette and with a half turn and curl of her fingers, the door of the front-loader opens. Fishing her only dollar note out of her back pocket, she takes it to the vending machine. She feeds it in and watches as the corner of the detergent box crushes against the glass as it sticks halfway down.

Fuck, she thinks. *God fucking damn it.*

She leans her forehead against the glass, one hand coming up to hold Chuckle's paws, her eyes closing as a heavy sigh rips its way from her chest.

I should be better than this, she thinks. *But I'm not better than this.*

She curls her fingers into a circle and flicks them out toward the stuck box.

It falls.

It's not the magic she has a problem with. Doing magic is second nature at this point. Normal. The only good thing that came out of her shitty childhood was that particular gift from her mother. It's just…the rest of it. Andy had never known self-doubt. Not until this past year, without the crutch of alcohol to soothe over her nerves. But the laundry is never-ending, and the dishes pile up, the bills grow steadier with every late payment, and she hasn't touched her guitar in months.

Andy breaks the cardboard seal as she walks to the machine.

She starts the cycle, placing half of her coins into the slot and pushing it in with a satisfying *thunk*. She moves over to the bench, unwinding Chuckle from around her shoulders and depositing him onto it. He mews in discontentment. She sits next to him. He tumbles blearily into her lap, eyes barely open, and is asleep again in seconds. Her fingers itch. Andy takes the cigarette from her lips and taps the ash out into the half-filled ashtray sitting in the middle of the bench. She looks at it for a long moment, the smouldering tip eating away at the paper dangerously close to her knuckles, and stubs it out in the tray. She reaches for her bag again, fingers catching on the badges dotting the strap as she pulls it against her hip. She rummages around inside until her fingers close over the cool metal of her chip.

'To Thine Own Self Be True' it reads proudly, curved around an embossed 'I'.

One year.

She rubs her fingers over the design, and the itch subsides.

She pulls out her Discman and a fresh cigarette from the crumpled pack. She flicks her BIC, lights the end. The opening chords of 'Planet Telex' begin to play as she sighs out around the smoke. She watches the liquid and cloth turn over each other, going around and around and around. She sucks in a mouthful of smoke, inhales it into her lungs and holds it there for a long, still moment. She exhales. The chip rolls over the knuckles of her other hand. She can't look away. The world shrinks in that moment.

There is nothing but the spinning, and the smoke, and the music, and the water.

It's raining.

Cold.

There's noise, coming from everywhere. *Bang-clatter-crash.* Rain. Sirens. Screaming. It's loud. So loud.

I'm in an alleyway, somewhere. Probably, maybe, I think. There's a big metal dumpster, the side dented and covered in peeling layers of paint, and graffiti, and paint to cover the graffiti. I dart for it, cowering behind the rust-covered front wheel. Shivering.

Cold.

The rain beats against the dumpster in a dull *thud-thud-thud-thud.* There are shadows here, dark enough to swallow up anything smaller than them. I'm swallowed. Scared.

There is this tug in my belly. Something different than the hunger pangs. I'm used to the hunger pangs. It's magnetic. Something tidal, ebbing under the call of the moon. It's so dark, buildings

136

shoot up from the ground and cover any hope of a silver light. Forsaken.

Rain pours.

Moon hides behind the comfort of clouds.

Something...someone is humming. Or, actually, not humming but murmuring. Chanting.

Calling.

It tugs at me. I crave it. Them. More than the hunger pangs. More than the fear of the rain.

I close my eyes. The tug is so strong now. I want to follow.

The rain pelts down.

I step into it. Eyes closed.

I'm so afraid. Eyes closed. I walk.

I don't know why I'm going. I don't know where.

I'm so hungry. I'm so cold. I'm so...

Alone.

Maybe that's why.

Eyes closed. I walk.

I see her anyway, the guiding light. So bright against the creeping blackness of the night.

She's sat, folded on the sidewalk.

She sits in a puddle of rainwater and chalk; her hair is plastered to her forehead in tangled clumps. My eyes are closed.

I see her still.

I know her. I would know her anywhere. I would know her in any place, under the cover of darkness, under the sweet smell of rain. I know her through time and circumstance. Her heart is my heart, her breath my breath.

I know her in my bones.

She is mine, and I am hers. Of this, I am sure.

Andy's eyes snap open, and it's like the walls of the laundromat whistle away from her at breakneck speed. There's a pounding behind her eyes and against her temples. Her chip falls to the ground with a clatter of metal against linoleum.

What the fuck?

What. The. Fuck?

She takes the cigarette from her lips, fully burned to filter, and drops it into the ashtray. As she reaches down to pick up her chip, she notices the trembling of her hands. She rubs her fingers over the embossing, and the rushing in her ears quells, if only slightly.

She remembers that day. How could she not? She remembers summoning Chuckle to her, desperate against the loneliness clawing through her lungs and chest. The way he had appeared, as if from nowhere, two pounds sopping wet with a tail stuck bumper-car straight; how his pale orange fur was ragged, licked up at the neck.

The angle was all wrong, though, she was somewhere too close to the ground. Like looking in a mirror at a carnival, or through the glass in an aquarium; something warped and unforgiving.

She looks down at her lap, Chuckle curled up in it. She can't bring herself to wake him, yet. Even with the rippling anxiety, she can't bring herself to voice the fear. Even though that's what he's there for. Her free hand scratches into his fur. She takes a deep breath. Whatever she just saw…well, it isn't important. She has to believe it isn't.

The washing machine clicks off.

She itches for another cigarette.

Her fingers tighten in Chuckle's fur, and she rolls the chip around her other hand. Her heart thumps in her chest an anxious beat. She tilts her head and the washer door swings itself open. Her clothes stutter through the air and into the tumble dryer. The remaining coins slot themselves into the machine and begin the drying cycle.

Andy shifts and tries to shake herself free from the panic that has been collecting in the hollow of her throat. Chuckle blinks a single eye open and looks at her for a long moment.

'You're nervous,' he thinks to her.

She quirks a lip. He always could tell. Andy tucks her chip into her pocket, careful as anything, and pulls her journal from her bag, resting it on top of Chuckle.

'Undignified,' he thinks, *'but okay.'*

She starts scribbling on the page; she draws a handful of stars, and scrawls down a few ideas for songs before she replies. *'Had a vision, I guess? Or a really fucked up flashback. Or a fantasy. A dream. A sudden onset panic-induced delusion. Some weird-ass magic bleed. I dunno.'*

The dryer beeps, finished. She clicks her fingers and fresh, warm clothing trails from the hatch, folding itself in the air and landing neatly back in the basket.

'C'mon,' she thinks as she shoos Chuckle from her lap. He stretches and jumps onto her shoulders, settling in for the two-block walk home.

The moon is hidden behind cloud and building; Andy's only guidance comes in the form of streetlamps that flicker overhead as she walks through each warm circle of light.

'Okay Chuckle-bug,' she thinks, pointing to the CD player as she nudges the door closed with her hip. The player clicks on and waits for a disc. Chuckle jumps down and pads into the kitchen.

Andy flicks her fingers toward the lava lamp in the living room as she passes by. It turns on and the room is bathed in a dim red, diffusing to a deep honeysuckle glow that reaches into the kitchenette.

Live Through This slides out from the disc tower. It opens, mid-air, and the disc slots itself into the player. Andy looks over and the play button pushes in. Courtney Love's vocals drift through the air as Andy places the washing basket onto her kitchen table.

She drops to the floor, cross-legged, and waits for Chuckle to meander his way over to her. She draws him into her lap, tracing a hand through the sherbet strands of his soft orange fur.

'Okay, okay, my kitty,' she thinks, tucking her face into the top of his head. The last of her anxiety, the unsettling paranoia seeping around the edges of her periphery, bleeds out. He leans into her, purring.

Andy smiles to herself, fond, and scratches behind his ear. He jumps from her lap as she moves to stand, and she picks him up, depositing him onto the table with her laundry.

'It's been a day, hasn't it?' she thinks, and the amber globed lamp in the corner clicks on as she walks past, into the kitchenette. *'Dinner time, hm?'* she looks over her shoulder at him, *'What do you say? Wanna be my little sous chef?'*

The look Chuckle levels at her is nothing short of withering. He bats at the basket; it inches toward the edge. She laughs. He jumps from the table and pads from the room.

The night grows heavier around her, darkness resting on her shoulders with all the weight of the sky itself. Sometimes, only in those looming hours of the night, it's like the walls of Andy's little apartment bend inward. They press on her, impending and immovable, until she finds herself sitting shoulder-to-shoulder with the cracks in the plaster. The room gets so small Andy thinks she might just burst out of it, exploding through the windowpanes, from the cracks under the door, through the pipes and the plugs.

A crack of lightning, unexpected and sharp white, cuts a streak across the stars. Andy jumps, dropping the fork onto the ceramic of her plate. Thunder does not follow, and nor does rain. She pulls from her pocket her one-year chip. Rolling it over her knuckles eases the racing of her heart.

She projects her mind to Chuckle, beckoning him the only way she knows how.

But he does not come.

'Chuckie,' she thinks, *'I need you here, please.'*

But he does not answer.

'Chuckle-bug?' she thinks, her feet rooted in place. She can't breathe, the air in the apartment stolen by the closing walls. Still, he does not answer.

Tears, unbidden and unwelcome, swell but do not fall. 'Chuckle!' she calls, forcing her voice to expel from tightened throat.

She's answered only by the sound of Chuckie jumping from her bed, his soft paws sound on the hardwood floor as he slinks down the hall. He winds around her ankles and stares up at her.

'Chuckle-bug, you come when you're called,' she thinks to him. He does not respond. She looks at him, and he looks back. Then, he opens his mouth and meows, singular and piercing. Andy feels a sudden rush of vertigo and has to press a hand to her sternum to stave off the nausea creeping through her diaphragm.

Quiet.

It's not been quiet in a long time.

I'm not sure what to do with all of the silence.

I have all these memories, but I don't think they're mine. I don't know her name.

I think I used to.

She has no fur, and she does not look like me, but I know we are the same. She leaves every morning, and I miss her. She comes home every night, and I miss her still. Even from the same room. Even worlds apart.

I think I will spend the rest of my nights longing for her. Sometimes I don't know where I end, and where she begins. It's so quiet.

I don't think I want to.

I'm meshed into her, so tangled that I couldn't find a way out if I wanted to.

I don't want to.

Why would I want to?

I know her in my bones, though I don't remember why.

She takes care of me. Good care of me.

That's enough.

We are still alive. Still alive, and under the same water. Whatever she is drowning in, I sip from. She is made from every part of me.

I don't remember why.

Andy blinks, pressing the heels of her hands into her eye sockets as her head throbs, just like in the laundromat. What is happening to her? What is this overwhelming sense of sadness, of loss? It settles into her lungs, heavy, like water to a drowned man, like hunger during a famine. It's something she has to carry with her, now, of this she is sure. She feels the sting of tears and wills them away. He has never meowed to her before.

'...*Chuckle?*' she thinks, to no response.

'Chuckle?' she says, and he lifts his head in turn. His head tilts to the side, and a wash of cold drips over Andy. 'Chuckie can you...can you not speak with me anymore?'

He chirrups, confused.

She picks him up and holds him at eye level, examining him with a devout sort of focus. When she is done, she draws him to her chest and holds him close.

There are no words there, she decides. He has no words left for her.

It's then, in a silence she hadn't been privy to since she first called for Chuckle eight years prior, that the tears still skirting the edges of her vision begin to fall in earnest.

Andy sobs until her chest is tight with it, heaving, wracking, shuddering through the entirety of her frame. How could she go on without Chuckie in her head? He'd been a constant part of her for so many years; a deep comfort, a solace for when the beckoning call of darkness dripped over her. He was supposed to be with her always.

And he is, that's the worst part.

He's still right there, in her arms where he belongs, rubbing his head to the underside of her jaw, batting at her chest.

But his voice, that's what was gone.

Andy sucks in a breath that ripples its way through her. She can't bring herself to put him down, even though she's sure he'd be getting sick of being held by now. She carries him down the hall and into her bedroom. She goes over to her desk and reaches into the drawer, manoeuvring the tricky false bottom one-handed and pulls free her grimoire.

They walk to the loungeroom, and Andy gestures for the CD player to turn on. She's never been one for silence. She collapses onto the couch with Chuckle settled on her lap.

As *Sparkle and Fade* lifts from the tower and begins playing softly, she pours over the writing in the book, a cacophony of handwriting crowding the margins with notes and advice. Her mother's hand, her aunt's, her own. There is no mention in any of it of a witch losing her soul-bond to her familiar.

The hours wear thin. The weak, sickly stream of the winter sun begins to ooze through her window in a pale trickle, fighting against the grey clouds and dim dawn. Andy sighs, stretching out her limbs. She's no further than when she'd started. Her best idea is to resummon him, but that is still just a guess. The joints of her elbows crack with a satisfying pop. She shakes herself loose and looks down at Chuckle. She has never loved another being anywhere close to the amount that she loves him.

They are the same in every sense of it. He is all she needs.

And she needs him back in her head. Her fingers itch. For the first time in months, she does not reach for her chip. She rubs at her eyes again, the beginning of a headache throbbing against her temples, and takes a moment to watch the fireworks glimmer and die behind her eyelids. She breathes in, holds it, holds it, and lets it out.

'Okay, Chuckle-bug, I think we're going to have to think practically,' Andy tells him, all pragmatism and clean teeth, 'because theory is getting us nowhere.'

She looks out the window.

The clouds had parted at some point, and now even the weakness of the sun washes over everything, glinting off the wet, blackish slush pooling in the gutters.

She thinks back to the memory from the laundromat; she thinks back to the skirting feeling from hours ago. Chuckle is her tether, her anchor to the world.

In the time before, Andy had been so lonely she almost didn't know how to live with it. Everything in her ached for some form of connection; for someone to talk to, someone to love. It felt like drowning with every day she spent alone, muddying through brackish water, only just buoyant enough to breathe. Chuckle had been the life-ring, a rope connected to the horizon line, guiding her to land. How will she be able to breathe again without him as her sentinel? If summoning him to her as a familiar once more doesn't work, will that be all that she would have left of him as she knew? Memories, or just feelings. A cat, but nothing more.

Would that be okay? Would she be okay?

She pushes him off of her lap, loathe as she is to be disconnected from him in a physical sense, and walks from the couch to the apothecary cabinet standing next to the CD tower. She rummages through each drawer, pulling free mugwort, dandelion, and sparrow-bone. She opens the topmost drawer and carefully takes out one of Chuckle's shed whiskers. She places all of the components into a small bag made of softened cheesecloth and holds it tight in her hand for a long moment.

She clicks her tongue at Chuckle, walking through the dimly lit lounge to the front door. She opens it, ignoring the hammering of her heart, and steps into the tired and sepia hall.

The wind smells clean tonight.

The moon is out, too. She lets me walk out of our home instead of holding me, something I haven't done in a long time. She follows me down the street.

I like her shadowing me. She doesn't let me slip too far from her.

She calls to me, using a word I don't understand, but know the shape of.

'Chuckle,' she says, and I know it's my name.

I pause. I turn back to her.

She sits in the centre of the sidewalk. I walk over to her and curl my way under her arm. I don't know why she's sat down.

I think as I press my head to hers, *'why are we stopping here?'*

She doesn't answer. I don't expect her to. Why should I?

Why would she?

She scoops under my belly. Her paw is hairless. Cold.

I let myself be moved.

The breeze bites against her skin. She shivers. She should grow some fur, then she'd be warmer.

She's making noise, but I don't understand her cries. She doesn't sound like me.

I feel like I should know what she's saying.

But I don't. I don't know why.

She sets me down in front of her and draws in white chalk around me. I sit still and let her. She places a bag in the circle with me, and I want to play with it, but her gentle paw stops me. I sit.

'*I'll be good,*' I think, and she doesn't reply. I wish she would.

She keeps on with her humming. Not humming, murmuring. Chanting.

Calling.

I don't know these shapes; I don't know these words. Her voice is calm as it rinses over me, but I can hear the shiver to the sound. I can hear the thickness of her voice.

I know her in my bones.

She is mine, and I am hers. Of this, I am sure.

Of only this, I am sure.

Lightning cracks. Sharp white. A streak across the stars splits the moon in half.

Thunder does not follow. And nor does rain.

'*Chuckle?*' Andy thinks and waits for a reply.

Slipping Through the Cracks

Mara Beltman

Belfast, Northern Ireland – 2015

Noah was supposed to be here by eight. For a moment I think he won't show, that he will bail on me and ignore the problem like he always does, and honestly, I can't even blame him. It would be so much easier if he just stopped talking to me altogether, treated me like a stranger, like we haven't just spent the past seven years being each other's person. I wouldn't put it past him to stoop so low. But knowing him, he's probably just trying to make a point by being late.

I don't expect him to be any earlier than nine.

Leaning against the worn yellow cabinets while I wait for the kettle to boil, an overwhelming sense of dread settles in the pit of my stomach, as if the faded floral walls of our apartment complex are closing in on me and there's no way of escaping it. It's a cold, sinking feeling I've grown to know all too well, waiting for him to show up, and not knowing when he will.

I pour hot water into two cups of instant coffee and look at the analogue clock hanging beside the fridge: 8:53pm. Should I even bother making him coffee?

Then, as if trying to prove me wrong, Noah walks through the doorway with slumped shoulders, pale cheeks and baggy eyes. The solemn look on his face makes my heart feel like it's been ripped out of my chest and crushed to pieces. I tell myself not to cave in, but given that we've spent the last five years living together and that I'm not some cold-hearted snake, I do what I assume any soon-to-be ex-girlfriend would do; I hug him.

'Sorry I'm late,' he says, side-hugging me back with one arm.

I try to ignore his cold demeanour. 'Don't worry about it. How have you been?' I ask, then cringe at myself for even asking it. Of course, the answer won't be: *oh, I'm great thank you, how are you?*

Noah shrugs his shoulders and pulls out a chair by the dining table, his stiff body sinking into the cushioned back, 'Oh, you know, as great as one can be in all of this.'

The mugs burn my fingers when I bring them over to the table. I notice the stack of coasters from the corner of my eye and hesitate. Do I choose peace today or do I choose violence? Already feeling on-edge, I go for the latter and place the mugs directly onto the mahogany table, paying no mind to the damage it may do. Noah raises an eyebrow, probably cursing me out mentally, and shakes his head. In about three seconds flat, he'll grab a coaster and place his mug on top of it. It's ironic, really, how much money we spent on this dining table though we never actually ate our food at it, and now, on the brink of breaking up, we finally decide to use it.

I wonder who will win the custody battle.

Noah places his mug on top of a coaster and pushes it off to the side, refusing to look me in the eye. My gaze drifts towards the letter stashed below a stack of books and I feel my stomach churn. I'll have to tell him at some point, but honestly, I'd rather throw myself down a staircase. It's almost easier to let him believe I don't love him anymore rather than have him know I went behind his back.

'So, are you going to say something, or are we just going to sit here in silence?' he mumbles, avoiding eye contact.

I watch him shaking from anxiety and too much coffee, and feel stumped about what to say. Am I making a mistake? I'm twenty-six now, and as my mother likes to remind me on every phone call, I'm not getting any younger. I wish I *was* still young, if only it meant I'd have my old self back. Maybe she would know what to do.

I know the right thing to do is tell him the truth, but instead I find myself saying, 'I don't even know where to begin.'

Noah wipes his palms over his face and mutters something under his breath: 'Fuck off, Chiara,' perhaps. I'm surprised he isn't yelling at me; it's not like I'm being very fair on him.

'I just don't understand Chi, I thought we were happy,' he says in a broken voice.

'We *were* happy, but we're not anymore,' I respond harshly, and instantly regret it when I see him physically recoil. He is looking at me now like I'm some sort of stranger and buries his face into his palms. I can tell he's trying not to cry.

'I thought you loved me, Chiara. I thought you were *in love* with me. You were once, right…in the beginning?'

'Of course I was Noah. I was so in love with you I was sick with it,' I say, stifling for a moment. 'Remember when we first moved into this apartment? I was so happy. I thought, from this moment on, I never want to spend another day apart from you.'

Belfast, Northern Ireland. 2010.

I was propped up on the mattress, smoking my third cigarette of the morning, and felt utterly overwhelmed. We'd moved into our flat the day before, and I already wanted to rip out the bloody kitchen. Apart from our lifetime supply of cardboard boxes and the mahogany table we purchased on a whim when driving through Boucher Road, the only other thing that occupied our one-bedroom apartment was a bright yellow kitchen, and in the short span of twenty-four hours it had already become my arch nemesis. It was as if someone had seen it in a seventies magazine and thought: *this is exactly what I want!*

Honestly, how could anyone ever want a yellow kitchen?

Balancing the cigarette between my chapped lips, I contemplated unpacking the box labelled 'bedroom' but the thought lost its momentum when I heard keys rattling in the front door. Stretching out my foot, I pushed the window sash higher and flicked out the cigarette.

'Hello, beautiful,' Noah said, kicking off his shoes.

I tucked my knees into my chest and looked at him, smiling widely.

'How was your morning?'

'Oh, you know, *so* fun when you have to get up at seven and deal with cocky clients.'

I gave him a smug look, 'Aren't you the cocky one though, working in finance?'

'Is that so?' he craned his neck, leaning over me. His thumb was pressed to my chin and turned my face towards him.

The space between us suddenly felt foolish, insubstantial. I wished for it to shrink, for us to be closer. He bent forward and my limbs turned to mush. If this was how living with him would be, I never wanted to spend another day apart from him. His fingers traced along the bones of my hip, sending shivers down my spine. My mouth was drier than the Sahara Desert and just when I thought he was about to kiss me, his fingers jabbed deep into the side of my stomach. A shriek escaped my lips. I dug my fingers into his shirt and pulled him down, the scent of his cedarwood aftershave consuming me. Laughing, I wriggled out of his grasp and knelt over him, my thighs pinning down his hips.

The way Noah was looking at me then made my heart skip a beat. His eyes spoke to me more than anyone else ever had. They said: I know every inch of who you are. We could talk for hours without saying any actual words.

Noah's hands settled on the curve of my back, pulling me towards him inch by inch. His thumbs dug into my hips, curling me into him like our bones were intertwining. He looked down at my mouth, our lips brushing against one another, then pulling apart. I felt like I was melting beneath his gaze and just as suddenly his lips were against mine.

A nervous breath stammered out of me, releasing the tightness within my chest. Placing a palm upon my cheek, I nestled myself within the warmth of his touch, my heart feeling light as his breath made its way into my lungs.

'I love you,' he whispered into my mouth.

Belfast, Northern Ireland. 2015.

Noah is slumped down with his head resting on the table. He's silent. I can tell he's contemplating what to say. The heels of my hands are pressed against my temples, trying to get rid of a developing headache. *This is going to be a long night.*

Beside the kettle is a cheap bottle of wine I bought for Noah and I think about drinking some. Perhaps it'll take some of the edge away. I stand up rather abruptly, the cheap IKEA chair screeching over the laminate floorboards, and walk over to the wine bottle, pouring myself a glass. I don't stop until it's filled to the brim and then gulp down half of the wine.

'What are you doing?' Noah asks.

'Having some shiraz—why, you want some?'

'This is not a conversation we should be having with alcohol.'

I pour some more shiraz into the glass. 'I beg to differ.'

'Turn on the kettle,' he orders, leaning backwards, 'I'd prefer tea.'

'You haven't even touched your coffee.'

'Did I ask for coffee?'

He's trying to get on my nerves with his snippy comments and instead of ignoring them like I usually do, I decide to play along. *Two can play at this game,* I think and aggressively flick the kettle on again. I snatch Noah's cold coffee from his hands and throw it down the drain, the kettle slowly beginning to boil.

Noah clears his throat. 'You cheated on me, didn't you? I mean, it's the only obvious answer. You don't touch me anymore, not like you used to, and you're always staying *behind* at work!'

'*What?*' I snap my head towards Noah, feeling anger boiling inside of me. 'You can't be serious!'

'You heard me. You cheated. Why else would you say no? I know you're hiding something from me so there's no point denying it.' He crosses his arms like he's proud of himself.

'Oh, so you and Olivia going on a work trip together without telling me is okay but the moment I do something wrong I *must* be cheating because there's no other possible explanation!'

'The difference is I can be trusted to spend a weekend away with a *colleague!*'

157

I'm too exhausted to deal with him so I ignore his comment, noticing the picture frame behind him perched up against some books in the shelf. My arms are wrapped around his, holding him tightly. He's right, I don't touch him anymore…not like I used to. In the photo there's a 'sold' sticker on the board behind us showcasing the one-bedroom unit in the heart of Belfast city—the kind of thing I never imagined myself owning at such a young age. My stomach drops; the happy girl in the picture feels like a stranger to me now.

'I didn't cheat on you,' I say and take the wine glass back to the table, the kettle still simmering.

'So, what? You just don't love me anymore? You're bailing on us? Going to pack up your things, move out, and that's it…we're done?'

'Don't say I'm giving up!' I snap. 'I've tried Noah…I really have. Do you know how many nights I've cried wishing I wouldn't feel this way?'

'Well why *do* you feel this way?'

My lip quivers. 'I don't know.'

'That's not good enough, Chiara!'

I look at the steaming kettle to avoid eye contact and blink away tears.

'Okay, fine—you want the truth? I *never* got to live the life *I* wanted. How can I get married and have kids with you when I'm fantasising about a life that you could never even give me!'

Noah's face drops. I can tell my words hurt him.

'Well what kind of life do you want, Chiara?'

'I don't know!'

'Yes, you do kno—'

'No! I don—'

'Tell me!'

'Everything in this relationship I've done for you, Noah. Have you ever thought about what I want? Did you ever even consider that I may not be happy? I gave up everything to be with you...to move here for you!' My voice chokes and I look towards the boiling kettle, its water almost spilling out.

'You and I both know we chose this life. You wanted us until you didn't—until you got bored. Don't fucking blame it all on me!' Noah snaps, his jaw clenched.

'I didn't choose this. I didn't choose any of this!' I yell, shoving the table away from me and jumping to my feet. The wine glass that was once half-full spills onto the table, staining it rich crimson red. It looks like a murder scene.

My chest rises and falls rapidly. I can't breathe nor contain my words and I physically feel the truth spilling out of me. 'I got accepted at Oxford, that's why I said no to you!' I yell and storm off to the bedroom, slamming the door shut behind me.

He opens the door and follows me into the room, 'You got accepted to *what?*'

'Oxford, a couple of weeks ago!'

'And you didn't care to tell me?'

'I didn't know what to say!'

'You didn't know what to say?' he laughs at this as if it's some hilarious prank. 'That's no fucking excuse, Chiara. I would've supported you. I would've gone with you!'

I sniff, mascara smudging my cheeks. 'No, you wouldn't have. You have a job here—a really good one for that matter—you would've never given it up. And if you were going to, I wouldn't have let you. I *won't* let you!'

Noah is crying now and reaches for my hand. He tugs at it, trying to pull me into him, but I don't let him. I push him away from me and he stumbles backwards like a lost puppy.

'No! You can't just kiss me and expect everything to get better.'

'I'll change, Chiara. I will. I'll quit my job, and we can move to England, and you can follow your dreams and—'

'That's not how this works.'

'But we can try!' tears are streaming down his face; I don't think I've ever seen him cry like this. 'You didn't even give me any signs. There's got to be a way we can make this work. I can't imagine my life without you!'

'I gave so many signs!'

'Well, I can't read your min—'

'I never wanted to marry you!' My words slap me in the face and then circle back and punch me in the gut.

Noah drops to his knees, whimpering, defeated by my words. He reaches for my legs and cradles them, sobbing into my calves. I try to escape his grip, but he won't let go.

'Please!' I cry, pushing onto his shoulders, 'please Noah, I don't want to marry you—I can't marry you. Please just let me go.'

Belfast, Northern Ireland. 2015.

I shuffled my bag higher onto my shoulder and prayed to God that for once the weather predictions weren't accurate. I was already an hour late; rain would only make it worse, and, knowing Noah, he was probably on the brink of combustion considering I hadn't let him know that I was asked to stay back at work.

Hurrying, I walked straight past the tarnished array of letterboxes and almost tripped over my own feet when my brain short circuited and stopped me in my tracks. I took three steps backwards and stood still, contemplating my next move. Surely, I wouldn't have received a response yet? I'd scrolled through countless of subreddits and almost all of them said that it would take up to two weeks to hear back from them...and reddit was never wrong.

Hooking the keys into the gap between my finger and thumb, I peered inside the box, scanning the envelopes. My organs felt like they were about to explode as I reached for the letter. It felt smooth against my skin and before I could even register the sender, I found myself tearing the envelope open.

I almost choked on my chewing gum.

The word **'ACCEPTED'** was bolded, underlined, and if that wasn't enough to bring the point across, it was capitalised as well. The word jumped out at me like my 2007 GCSE results and suddenly I felt like I was about to pass out.

This wasn't happening. Not right now.

Shoving the envelope deep into my coat pocket, I ignored the tingling sensation rising in my chest and sprinted up the stairs. Inhaling deeply, I pushed the door open with my foot and froze. Noah was there, dressed in the burgundy suit he bought last Christmas, sitting at the dining table, waiting for me. Pillar candles and a vase of flowers adorned the table with gold-plated dinnerware. He'd really gone all out. I felt like I was about to vomit.

'Here she is. Happy anniversary, darling,' he said, standing up.

I forced a smile, shoving the acceptance letter deeper into my pocket.

'What do you think?' he asked, gesturing towards the table.

'It's beautiful,' I lied, feeling sick with guilt.

'So, the plan is, you get changed, I surprise you with my gift, and then we have some dinner,' he smiled, though it did nothing to cover up his visible nerves. Was he upset that I was late?

In the bedroom, I slipped into the cherry silk dress I'd bought during High Street's winter sale two years ago and stood in front of the arched mirror, shoulders pushed back. My cheeks were blemished and the bags under my eyes looked like they were about to explode but at least I'd straightened my hair that morning. *Could be worse,* I thought and stepped into the living room.

Noah stood in front of the table; his back turned towards me. He was playing with something in his pocket and for a second it almost looked like a small box. I took a deep breath, trying to ignore the guilt that was eating me alive, and placed my hand onto the small of his back. He turned, eyes lighting up the moment they met mine. His hand slipped into mine and I felt nothing. Shouldn't this feel more special after seven years?

'You look beautiful,' he said, gently kissing my lips.

I didn't respond, I didn't know how to. All I could think of was the acceptance letter stashed in my pocket and how this life was becoming a living nightmare. I looked away, wishing to be anywhere but there.

His eyes flicked towards the ground. I couldn't breathe. His hand was still in his pocket and then just as suddenly it was pulling out a small velvet box. He dropped to his knee, holding out a silver ring. I couldn't feel my body. My heart was pounding so loudly I almost didn't even hear his next words.

All I could do was stare at the ring in his hand.

Belfast, Northern Ireland. 2015.

Noah is on the ground with his face stuffed into his hands, muffling his sobs. I'm sitting opposite him against the edge of the bed, cradling my knees into my chest to feel some sense of comfort. It's not like I can expect Noah to comfort me anymore.

I feel empty and wipe away my smudged mascara with my knuckle, thinking back to the first night we spent in our bedroom. If it wasn't for the fact that my insides felt like they were about to spew out of me, I would almost think I was dreaming, and that tomorrow I'd wake up in our bed like nothing ever happened. I consider the possibilities of what would happen if I stopped breathing and conclude that the following two things would happen: I would either wake up from this horrible nightmare just to be in another one, or I would simply die. I don't know which scenario is worse.

Noah gulps, breaking the silence. 'You were happy though, weren't you?'

My heart stings from his words, 'I was, I'm sorry,' I say, feeling guilty. 'I shouldn't have said that. It was uncalled for.'

'I'm sorry I yelled,' he says with a broken voice and all I want to do is hold him.

'It's okay. I don't blame you.'

'I just don't understand,' he wipes his palms over his tear-stained cheeks, 'what did I do wrong?'

'You didn't do anything wrong.' I pause, thinking of what to say next. 'I was never the marriage type of girl, you know that. I can't be in one place for too long, but then you got that promotion, so we stayed here, and I hated it. I'm not made for that stay-at-home life.'

'I think one day you'll find yourself thinking differently.'

'Maybe, but not now—'

'Not with *me*, you mean.'

'No—well *yes* but…not with anyone right now.'

'But maybe in the future?'

'Maybe someday.'

'But not with me.'

'No, Noah…not with you.'

There is a pause, a moment of silence and the room feels like it's been drained of all life. A cold lump of dread settles in the pit of my stomach and I pull my sleeves over my wrists.

Through the window, dark, thunderous clouds roll into the sky, twisting and turning into turmoil. Vigorous winds rush through the air like a vortex, deforming the trees and stealing their leaves. Nature has lost its colour and the flowers have withered. The world looks like it's decaying, like the Earth's core has stopped spinning.

'I'll always love you, you know that, right?' he mumbles, staring down at the carpet.

'I'll always love you as well.'

'But just not *in love* with me.'

I ignore his comment and rub my fingers together. All I can think of is being held by him. Does that make me selfish? I want to feel his warmth one last time, to savour it and store it in my lockbox of memories of him. On my knees, I scoot over to him and nudge him with my shoulder. He knows what I want, so he drops down onto his back. His stiff body falters the moment I lay my head down on his chest. I take in his heartbeat and his scent; he smells of his cedarwood aftershave and this is the last time I'll ever smell it again. He moves his arm and places it on the small of my back and I think, *I will miss you until the day I die.*

'Why didn't you tell me sooner?' he asks after a moment.

'Because I was scared. I didn't want to admit it to myself. I didn't want to face reality.'

'And the reality being leaving me?'

'*Hurting* you. I didn't—I *don't* want to hurt you.'

'Well, it's a bit too late for that.'

'Noah.' I lift my head and look at him, watching his chest rising and falling with every breath.

'I know, I'm sorry,' he shakes his head. 'It's not your fault.'

I move onto my knees and sit beside him, resting my back against the wall. He sits up too but doesn't look at me. We're getting close to the point of saying goodbye. I glance at him and notice his creased eyes are filled with sadness. I wish there was an easier way of breaking up with someone; I hate seeing him sad.

Trying to think of something funny, I say, 'Olivia has a thing for you, you know that, right?'

'Oh, come on Chiara, that is a foul thing to say.' He doesn't laugh, instead he looks even more hurt.

'Why? It's a compliment. Besides, I would be okay with it.'

'You would be okay with what?'

'With you and Olivia.'

This time Noah softly laughs. 'We haven't even broken up yet and you're already trying to set me up with other people.'

'But we *are* breaking up.'

'I know…I guess I'm just not ready to let you go yet. I'll miss you so much,' he puts his hand to his stomach, 'I'll be sick with it.'

I reach for his hand and hold it in mine, he doesn't let go. 'You will be at first, but I promise it will get better.'

He sighs hesitantly like he doesn't know whether he wants to say his next words. 'I think you should go, though,' he pauses and looks at his hands, 'regardless of how it'll affect me.'

I look at him and suddenly see the last seven years flash before my eyes. All the love, all the pain…everything. I know then, in that moment, that a part of me will never stop loving him, no matter how hard I try.

The Star-Set Elevator

Hayden Thomas

Lunar 1, The Moon – 2178 AD

I had always wondered what life was like among the stars. Ever since the first colony was established fifteen years ago, I'd dreamed of escaping to the moon.

As I stepped through the sliding door and into the most luxurious room I had ever seen, I finally got a taste of that dream. The room alone was bigger than my apartment on Earth. A piano sat in one corner; bookshelves lined the bleached walls. The far wall was entirely glass, a giant window looking out into the star-speckled void. The Lunar Elevator was barely visible through one of the window's corners. A giant rotating cylinder, it allowed quick travel between Earth and Lunar 1, so long as you could handle the G-force.

'Alix?' My voice echoed in the cold room as I treaded softly across a clean, untouched rug. A stark contrast to the soulless tiles that covered the rest of the medical sector. 'Alix? My name is Chip León, I'm from CareCare.' My voice echoed throughout the cold suite. The gravity here seemed even weaker than when I first stepped out of the Lunar Elevator.

A glass cover was fitted to each of the bookshelves, stopping the few remaining books from drifting off the shelves. I could see the dust lining each key as I passed by the piano. When I had met with Alix's parents before I left for the moon, they mentioned that Alix used to have lessons. It reminded me of my days as a medical student, when the present had meaning, and the future was promising. Days spent hidden away in our little college dorm, playing songs with Gabriella till our neighbours complained.

Bygone days.

Struggling to stay on the floor, I peered around a corner into a large, open kitchen. It was perfectly tidy and filled with fancy electronic appliances only the richest households could afford. I was happy to know I wouldn't be spending every day tidying up.

I could hear the faint drum of music. It crept from a door opposite from the kitchen. With big, light steps, I waded over to the door and knocked three times. There was a small red LED in place of a handle. After a moment, the light flicked green, and the door slid open silently.

The room was as pale as every other; dim white light illuminated it sparingly. The music was much louder than I expected. It sounded like a modern take on classic rock and roll, intense synthetic sounds almost drowned out the snapping drums.

The moment I stepped inside, the door sealed shut with a soft hiss.

The room was a mess. The bed was unmade, and drawers were left half-open, legions of light-blue jumpsuits spilling out. More notable, though, were the dozens of books that floated weightlessly around the room, among which I noticed a teenager, drifting towards the ceiling. They wore one of the jumpsuits, their half-rolled-up sleeves revealed skin wrapped tight around bone. It pained me to notice, but their condition was in plain view, the moment I saw them. I must have been standing there for a minute before they finally spoke up.

'Your badge,' they said as they pushed off the ceiling and floated between books, their head bopping to the beat. I thought it was reasonable to want proof of my identity, so I retrieved my badge from my pocket. My picture stared me down with tired eyes. It was like watching myself through a foggy telescope.

I realised too late that the gravity in this room had been modified to suit Alix's condition. I took a single step, and the momentum gently propelled me into the air. My badge slipped from my grip, swiftly drifting beyond reach.

'Hi, Alix. I'm—' I was already approaching a wall, headfirst. I raised my arms and prepared for collision.

'You're from the company, I know.' They began to spin as they descended to the floor. 'They told me you were coming. You really from Earth?' I found I couldn't see them anymore, my face was practically pressed against the wall.

'I just arrived maybe an hour ago. They didn't even give me a tour, you know.' I grabbed hold of a small lip on the wall and stabilised myself.

'Do you miss it? Being on Earth?' They sounded distant, as if they were trying to sound disinterested. I tried turning but lost my grip and started rotating horizontally.

'I was only there the other day, try asking again in a week.' I chuckled to myself, but the only response I heard was the continual thumping music.

Suddenly, when I was almost completely upside down, the wall in front of me slid to one side. I found myself staring straight at Earth, the swirling blues and whites half hidden behind a veil of darkness. A plain planet of discarded dreams.

'It's colourful, isn't it?' The music was still thumping as I stared at the celestial body. *Of course it's colourful*, I thought. *There's nothing special about that.* I finally managed to rotate away from the window. The books had been arranged in a large circle in the middle of the room. Inside it, Alix balanced on one hand, slowly spinning themselves. Their young eyes looked even more tired than mine.

'My name is Chip. It's nice to meet you, Alix.' My badge drifted slowly into my hand.

'Hi, Chip. Want me to show you around?'

As we strolled through the medical sector's bland corridors, we occasionally passed other people in blue jumpsuits. They would smile and wave at Alix, who would sometimes wave back and force a stiff smile. Our first and only destination turned out to be a kind of park in a ginormous bubble that I had spotted as I was escorted from the Lunar Elevator. Sitting on a bench, we had a simple, yet slightly bizarre conversation.

'Did you get to meet the last giant panda?' Alix asked.

'I was only a teenager then, but I did see her on TV,' I answered honestly.

'Okay, what about rivers, have you ever swum in one? Or in the ocean?'

'Of course, my family lived not too far from a river mouth, where the river meets the sea. We went spent every weekend swimming and soaking up the sun.' I could tell Alix was enjoying hearing about life on Earth. This time their smile was genuine, and I could see their eyes light up at each answer. I decided not to mention the now polluted waters that flowed out from that river.

'Do you plan on visiting Earth someday, Alix?' I was curious, as Alix's parents were living on Earth. The pair weren't the kindest of folks, so absorbed in their business that they had abandoned their only child, a horribly sick one at that, to keep their wallets filled. I had little respect for them, treating their child more like an inconvenience than a human.

'I've tried to get permission from everyone, and I've tried—' their voice lowered to a whisper, '— running away.' Alix slid their slip-on shoes back and forth across the smooth floor beneath the bench. 'But they just won't let me. It's like I'm a prisoner in this stupid place.'

'Well, the trip to Earth would be especially dangerous for you, I'm sure the doctors've got your best interests in mind.' The truth was that they did want to help, they just weren't willing to let Alix go when the risk was so high.

'They don't know though; I could make the trip to Earth perfectly fine.' There was a faint confidence in Alix's tone. I knew they desperately wanted to prove them all wrong.

'One day,' I said. 'Your parents will be waiting, I know it.' I smiled over at Alix, and they smiled back. That stiff smile they showed to the passers-by. I would never mention their parents again.

Weeks passed and the sun disappeared beyond the horizon. Everything cooled down, and life became warmed only by bright, white lights that dotted every ceiling and floor of the medical sector. Every other day I would take Alix from their living quarters to the musculoskeletal physician for therapy. It didn't take long for me to notice these were the days Alix truly despised. The doctors would have them lifting weights, stretching bands, and running treadmills until they were clearly in pain. I was informed of Alix's physical condition before I arrived on Lunar 1, but seeing them in such pain only reminded me of the tragedy of the situation. All this pain was only prolonging the inevitable.

Still, I kept a smile on my face, and tried my best to bring Alix happy moments in their constant struggle. Trips outside the medical sector, and endless stories of life on Earth, anything to distract them from the constant hurt.

While I did mention my time as a medical student, my hobbies, and my childhood, I didn't exactly tell a true story. I never mentioned why I abandoned my studies. Alix didn't need to know that I was reliving the worst weeks of my life by their side.

Watching that disease slowly take Gabriella, my family, my dreams, my everything...I wish I could have done more, done *anything*.

In those early weeks, I wasn't sure I could endure that pain again. But sitting there, celebrating my forty-fifth with Alix smiling beside me, I felt a part of that void fill.

There was joy, amongst that pain.

The following months flew by, and I started noticing some grey curls in my beard. When Alix wasn't showing me shortcuts around the medical sector or interrogating me about Earth, I was busy cleaning, cooking, or fetching groceries. Groceries were free when I got them for Alix, so I got experimental in the kitchen.

One morning, I asked Alix if they wanted to tag along on a trip to the market. They weren't too excited, but I insisted. They hadn't really explored much beyond the medical sector; the gravity was apparently 'too heavy.' The market's large dome was packet tight with buildings you'd see in the old European cities, and it was always the busiest area of the colony. After some brief shopping, we happened upon a small stall boasting a variety of cheese-based snacks.

'Do they have these on Earth?' With a raised eyebrow, Alix held up a mozzarella stick.

'Do you want to hear a secret?' I asked. They nodded and leant in, cupping one ear in their hand and looking around suspiciously. 'Most of this stuff is made on Earth and sent up here on the elevator.' Their eyes widened as they stared at the mozzarella stick. One mouthful later and that smile showed itself again. Alix didn't smile often, but when they did, it warmed my heart.

'So that's why they taste way more awesome than the normal food.' Alix said as they munched on their cheesy snack.

Staring up into space, I could just barely see Earth over the rooftops. It was so far away. 'I knew that already, though,' I heard, obviously a bluff. I turned, and Alix was also staring up at Earth, massaging their legs grumpily.

'Time to head back?' I asked.

'Yeah, my back's super sore.' We turned around and began the walk back home. Alix stopped at every window and dome, trying to get a view of the Earth, even leading me off course to see it from one of the park bubbles. I told them to be careful, that they could see it from their room. They told me to mind my own business.

All that running had left Alix hugging a wall, clearly struggling to stand. In the end I hoisted them up, slung one arm around my shoulders, and we walked back together. I could tell Alix was embarrassed. Still, I couldn't help but lend a hand. I never really believed Gabriella when she said it was the little things that mattered, but in that moment, I knew just how important those things were.

When we finally got home, Alix could relax, and I could get started on dinner.

'You shouldn't wear yourself out like that, you know it can catch up on you real quick,' I was making sure they knew I cared. It had the wrong effect.

'Yeah, of course I know. It's all I know.' They drifted, dejectedly, towards their bedroom.

'I'm just looking out for you. It's just that...' My thoughts evaded me.

'I get it. I'm not allowed to do stuff everyone else can do.' They had almost reached their door.

'I know it's not fair—'

'Yeah, it's not. I have to watch the other kids run around and have fun from my window in this stupid medical sector, locked in this horrible place while everyone else gets to go and live their lives.' Tears began to flow as Alix drifted through their open door. I followed quickly.

The wall was transparent, and we could both see out into space. It looked as though Alix was floating free, their tears glimmering like little stars.

'I want to get out,' they said. 'I want to go to that crazy planet you always talk about. I...' They looked out into space, towards Earth, as they landed gently on the ceiling.

'I want to see my parents, but...'

A long pause. A silence so deep I felt I was drowning.

'I'm already so tired. I can hardly get to the doctor myself, how am I supposed to get to Earth?' I drifted further into the room and floated among the books as Alix spoke, gazing out into space. I could see the Lunar Elevator reaching its lone limb out to Earth—its twisting cylindrical body was so unnatural, so out of place.

This whole colony was Alix's prison. A part of me wanted them to escape.

'I know it's difficult, but you can't let your condition take you prisoner. Over these past months I've seen what makes you...you. It's everything beyond the physical therapy and the days spent stuck inside.' I flapped my arms and moved slowly towards Alix. 'It's your love for books, that thirst for the unknown, and the pizza nights. Plus, I'll always be here if you need, whether you like it or not.' This time I did get a chuckle. As they drifted close, I noticed a smile.

'Maybe you're right. I shouldn't let my weird muscles hold me back.' They flexed their arms and let out a relieving laugh. 'I can do *anything*.' I was a little caught off guard. I didn't think I was that convincing.

'Do you...need a hug?' I put those doubts aside. I felt that if it were me, I'd need a hug.

'Bleh.' Alix stuck out their tongue. 'No way, dude.' A book smacked into my head. Alix chuckled, still wiping tears. 'Now get outta here and make me some Bolognese!'

'I'll let you know when it's ready, Your Majesty.' I closed the door behind me. I felt a little bad, like I should've done better. I couldn't subdue my doubts.

It was a quiet dinner; we didn't talk. Eventually, Alix took their bowl into their room, and I sat alone at the table. It wasn't my best Bolognese.

I hardly slept that night, after the colony's lights went out and the constant whirring dulled. Hours passed as I turned and wriggled in my sheets. I had a terrible feeling in my gut, but I ignored it. Of course I ignored it. Eventually, I drifted away into my subconscious and left my worries for when I awoke.

In my sleep I heard the soft notes of classical piano in the distance. It reminded me of home, and of my old life.

It was maybe a year before Gabriella passed. We spoke about our future, sat together on the couch by the window. Rain pattered soft on the glass, droplets streaking down, racing one another. She mentioned children, and how much she wanted them. We had been together for years by then, but I just wasn't ready. So, I pushed it aside. In the future, when life's settled, I thought.

I will always dream of what could have been.

Sweat clung to my forehead as I jolted up. The quiet buzz of the colony's artificial day had returned. I switched on the lights as I drifted out into the foyer. Immediately, I moved to the piano and could clearly see a lack of dust.

'Alix?' I called out, approaching their bedroom door. The LED was green, the door was unlocked. I thought that fairly odd, but didn't want to intrude. 'Rise and shine,' I continued as I checked my watch. 'I'll cook up some eggs. It's already half past nine.'

No response.

I scratched my beard, looking out through the foyer's glass wall. Barely in view, the elevator's segments spun slowly, like they always would before a shuttle was sent to Earth. 'I was thinking you could…' Each segment of the elevator twisted in unison, like the cogs in the heart of a clocktower '…practice some piano.'

Alix's door slid open, revealing the horror of my situation. The room was tidy. No book was out of place in the shelves, the bed was made perfectly, and there were no clothes spilling from the drawers. The bedroom's transparent wall revealed the Lunar Elevator, still spinning, pointed straight at Earth.

The white halls rushed by as I raced around corners and through doorways. I recalled a stairwell Alix had told me about, a shortcut in the direction of the Lunar Elevator's Ground Floor, the factory-like boarding station where the shuttles slip up into the elevator and out into space. It was at the centre of the colony, not too far from the medical sector. My aging body hadn't endured more than a jog in years, but I knew the pain I was feeling was nothing compared to Alix's everyday life. So, I ran, out the medical sector and past a variety of Moon residents, until finally I made it through the hefty doors and onto the Ground Floor.

Looking around, I quickly noticed Alix propped up against a metal pillar, a few metres from the Elevator's entrance. A thrum of people queued at the small door, a group that Alix could disappear into at any moment. I made my way around the circular outer wall of the room, avoiding a large crowd gathered to see their friends and family off, before approaching Alix.

I didn't want to draw attention; it would only complicate something I could resolve myself.

'Attention passengers, the shuttle will disembark in two minutes!' an announcement blared. My heart was pumping as I made it to Alix.

'Alix.' I crouched down, getting on their level. We were only metres from the queue.

'Let me leave.' Alix was breathing heavily; they must have been so sore.

'This…this is crazy, just think about—'

'No, this isn't crazy. It's my life.'

'Alix, listen to me, this is dangerous. You know what could happen. You know what might come next.'

'*My* life is what comes next. It's *my* life, and *my* decision. I don't even care if I don't make it.' This was the freedom that Gabriella never had. The freedom to choose. But it shouldn't have come to this.

A loud beep sounded, and I glanced over at the queue of passengers. The door had opened, and they were beginning to file in quickly. Alix looked over too. My head was spinning.

'It's always been 'eventually'. Eventually you'll see the world. Eventually you'll get stronger. Eventually you'll get to *live*. I'm sick of the lies, and I'm sick of this place. I can't wait anymore. I want to live, to be free. Please, Chip, please let me go.'

Tears streaked down their face. The line of passengers collapsed into a muddled group. The crowd was shrinking, I knew the onlooking people could see us.

'How could I live with myself, letting you go?' I could feel it in my beating heart. In my shaking hands. In my clenched teeth. The fear of losing someone else.

'The same as before, the same as always. A new client, a new place,' Alix pleaded. I covered my face. I couldn't. After this, it all ends. They wouldn't make it to Earth. They wouldn't be with their parents. And the world would blame me, punish me for letting them go. But I couldn't tell them that. How could I tell them it wouldn't work out; what right did I have?

In the end, I truly hope that Alix thought they would make it to Earth. That they wanted a new life, not just an escape from this one.

'It's your choice,' I muttered. 'If you want to take a chance at a life on Earth. If you want to…' I was on my knees, and for the second time in my life, I began to cry into my hands, '…be with your parents, despite it all. It's your decision to make.' I was torn to shreds. I knew Gabriella would have wanted that choice.

I felt a hug, a brief embrace.

'Thank you,' Alix said.

And I felt them let go.

I could hear the Elevator begin its launch sequence. The shifting pressure of the shaft sealing shook the room's cold floor. I lowered my hands from my face to stare up as the shuttle rose out from the surrounding structure and into the Elevator's shaft.

I looked among the crowd, maybe Alix had changed their mind. But I only saw cheerful strangers, waving happy goodbyes to their loved ones. A group I could never be part of.

Behind them, I saw a group of security officers by the entrance. I didn't care what happened here, anymore. What was done, was done. I didn't doubt for a second that Alix was finally free.

Through the glass ceiling I finally saw Earth's colours. They were truly indescribable. Thank you, Alix. It was a bittersweet, beautiful symphony.

You would have loved it, Gabriella.

Acknowledgments

Attachment Theory began its life as an anthology themed around reincarnation. When that idea died, it was reborn into the collection it is now, an exploration of love—selfish and selfless; platonic, familial, and romantic; love that lasted a lifetime and love that lasted just a little while. Throughout the course of writing, editing, and working together not just for this anthology but over the three years of our undergraduate degree, we as a collective have forged a bond that will last a lifetime.

We would like to thank Dr. Amy Matthews for her guidance and compassion over the years. Without you we would be lost at sea, orphaned by barbarians, beheaded by the king, eaten by a horse. Thank you for always looking out for us, and for being a source of inspiration, laughs and invaluable advice. We will be indebted to you for the rest of our lives, and grateful for it too.

Additionally, we'd like to extend a massive thank you to Lynette Washington and Glimmer Press for their continued support of the Flinders Anthology classes past and present. Thank you for your patience, kindness, and immeasurable hard work. We'd also like to thank Abby Guy, for both helping to kick off the Flinders Anthology class back in 2021, and for designing the cover art for our book.

To Dr. Sean Williams for being not just a teacher but a friend, and for being a sounding board for title ideas and story concepts. Even though you gently suggested scrapping the reincarnation idea at the last minute and left us scrambling to catch up, it was the call we needed to hear. To Dr. Lisa Bennett for being a shining star in our lives. Even though sometimes we can't see you, when we can we're always looking at you in awe. To Dr. Nick Prescott, we love and miss drinks at the Tav with you. We'll always be grateful for your passion and enthusiasm in classes. Thank you all, for everything.

To Flinders University for funding the anthology, and for allowing us this incredible opportunity to learn and grow while holed up in various rooms all across campus.

We'd also like to thank our friends and families for their grace, love, and support as we stressed over deadlines and finding meeting times that worked for everyone. A specific thank you to Emma Pearce—a close friend of many of us—for sitting in on our editing sessions and reminding us of the basics when we got too lost in the weeds.

Finally, we would like to thank each other. This group has been a blessing. We thank each other for our hard work; for the patience and understanding; for the baked goods and matcha KitKats brought to share at meetings that kept us going. We thank Mara Beltman, Penny Foster and Indigo James for their diligence at social media marketing—running both a

TikTok and Instagram page can't be easy! Thank you to Travis Abrook and Maddy Nyp for their work as corresponding editors. Thank you to the rest of our editing team: Jesse Allan, Rachel Bauer, Ez Knill, Hayden Thomas, and Gavin Vouriot.

We did it, guys!

Author Bios

Travis Abrook

Travis Abrook is a historical fantasy author based in Adelaide, South Australia—a soon-to-be graduate of Flinders University with a Bachelor of Creative Art's Creative Writing. Travis thrives on his plot and his world-building in creating rich, beautiful fantasy worlds. Since Travis was young, he has always watched and adored his mother's interest in the fantasy world, that is reading fantasy books, such as *Cradle* by Will Wight. Travis, in turn, one day hopes to write a large fantasy selection similar and to have his mother read this epic fantasy series.

Jesse Allan

Jesse Allan is here, too. This soon-to-be graduate of Flinders University's Creative Writing BCA has lived all their life—and will probably die—in Adelaide. They take inspiration for contemporary and psychological horror from their lived experience and have a particular love for poetry. This historical narrative is a major outlier from most of their work, but it too exists, and is an example of their love for writing about the complexities of the human experience.

Rachel Bauer

Rachel Bauer has been telling stories from a young age, with a focus on making the uncommon, common. She writes as widely as she reads, translates Japanese webnovels into English, and is an avid collector of esoteric knowledge. She has co-written for an indie TV pilot, written a piece for an Adelaide Fringe show, and will soon finish her writing degree at Flinders University.

Mara Beltman

Mara Beltman is an emerging writer with a passion for contemporary fiction that explores the complexities of the human experience. Originally from The Netherlands, she traded tulips for gumtrees and now calls the sunny state of South Australia home, where she has completed a degree in Creative Arts (Creative Writing) at Flinders University. When she is not lost in her writing, she's likely curled up on the couch with a book in hand and cats on her lap.

Penny Foster

Penny Foster is an inspiring dyslexic writer who is currently finishing her bachelor's degree in creative writing at Flinders University. Originally from the growing seaside town/city of Victor Harbor, she has always wanted to write and create entertainment for others. When she is not writing with a cup of tea next to her-English breakfast, she is using her maladaptive daydreaming to conjure up more stories and more ideas.

Indigo James

Indigo James is a contemporary fiction writer based in South Australia. She is a recent graduate of a Bachelor of Creative Arts, Creative Writing at Flinders University. Indigo has a fondness for dark romance and psychological thrillers. Initially trained as an astrologer, she now incorporates her knowledge of the stars into her writing.

Ez Knill

Ez Knill is an up-and-coming author born and raised on the Lefevre Peninsula, who has completed a bachelor's degree in creative writing from Flinders University. They have a focus on poetics and magical realism, a keen interest in the beauty of the mundane, and a love for the atmospheric over the plot-heavy. Their longer-form fiction pieces have been described as 'basically just extended poetry' by their mother.

Maddy Nyp

Maddy Nyp is an aspiring author from the small town of Highland Valley, and a recent graduate of Flinders University with a BCA in Creative Writing. She is a novelist, scriptwriter and lyricist, with an interest in writing mystery and fantasy fiction. She enjoys tackling themes of environmental change and mental health. Maddy has previously worked with Writers SA on their zine *This Breath*, and has published several short stories through their organisation. When Maddy isn't writing, she is looking after her emotionally needy Alaskan Malamute, Cash.

Hayden Thomas

Hayden Thomas is a young writer born and raised in Adelaide. While completing a Bachelor of Creative Writing at Flinders University, he developed a love for the short story form and for all things fantastical and sci-fi-ish. If nothing else, he hopes to spend his life interrogating creative conventions and sharing his stories with the world.

Gavin Vouriot

Gavin Vouriot is a young writer and lover of fantasy and science-fiction. He is based in South Australia, but was born in Vancouver, Canada. He has completed a Bachelor of Creative Arts (Creative Writing) at Flinders University and enjoys reading, watching, and playing stories in a wide variety of genres. He aims to write fiction for middle-grade and young adult audiences.